QUEEN OF THE STARS

BOOK ONE

USA TODAY BESTSELLING AUTHOR

CATHERINE BANKS

QUEEN OF THE STARS

1

THEIR FAE GODDESS

Queen of the Stars by Catherine Banks.

Cover design by Ana Cruz Arts.

Published by Turbo Kitten Industries.

www.CatherineBanks.com

Turbo Kitten Industries™, P.O. Box 5012, Galt, CA 95632

ACKNOWLEDGMENTS

Thank you to the following people who helped make this book possible:

R.J. for answering all of my questions, telling me when I'm being ridiculous, and helping me keep sane amongst all the craziness that is involved with being an author.

C.R. for allowing me use her as a guinea pig and turn her into a RH fan. Also, for helping me with tasks that I would otherwise forget.

Lea for being my beta reader and allowing me to bounce ideas off of her constantly. And, to keep me straight on what is going on.

Jenica for being the bestest, helping me during my rough spots, and just existing.

As always, my amazing husband and best friend, Avery. Without you, this dream would not be possible. I can't wait until our joint dream comes true. The current dream I'm living in is pretty dang good as is, though.

Thank you also to my amazing Kickstarter supporters:

Alicia Rades
Andromeda Taylor-Wallace
Annette McElroy
Betheny Thompson
Brooke
Candace Wondrak
Christina
Christina Hunt

Claire Ellison
Daniel Tice Jr
Derek Murphy
Helen Scott
Jacqueline Hayley
Jathan McBride
Kaiya Kagon
Jennifer Laslie
Jessica Paige
Jessica Robbins
Karri Allen
Altheda Rutherford
Kathy
Kristal Melton
Lance McKee
Leslie Twitchell
Marie Andreas
Mettie A.M.
Winter Bruno
Michael Green
Michelle McFarlin
Nikki Jefford
Sunny Side Up
Cali Mann
Rachel Strehlow
Shannon
Sky A Fallows
Stephanie Meier
Stuart March
Tanya
Wanda
Jaycee DeLorenzo

Minloa

Lenta

Silpo

Blustum

Crol

Menma

Adlin

Klinsot

Dead Lands

Treska

Eltare

Vlink

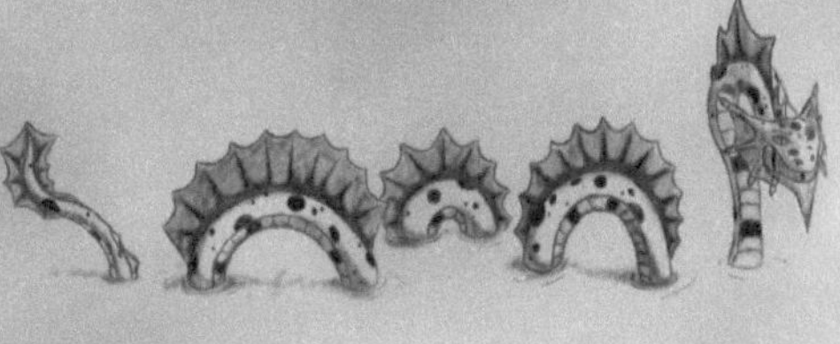

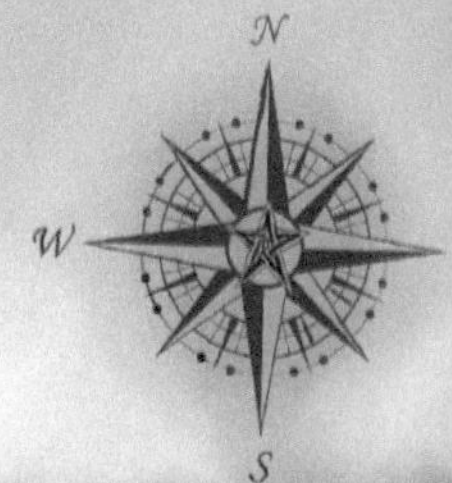

CHAPTER 1
ELARA

"STAY DOWN, or I'll break your arm," Quin growled at me.

Already on my hands and knees, I didn't know when to give up. Quin had challenged me, which pissed me off on its own, but then he'd made the match magic-free because he knew I sucked at hand to hand combat.

Slowly, I got to my feet and stood. I spat out sand, and glared at him. "You hit like a pixie." Taunting him wasn't smart, but my mouth had a mind of its own most days.

He snarled, revealing slightly pointed canines.

Raising my fists to defend myself, I prepared for his attack.

He lunged and ran into a mass of muscled perfection with the name Kydrus.

Quin leapt backwards, eyes wide.

Kydrus hadn't even looked at Quin. His eyes were focused on me. "This fight is over. Elara, come with me."

Quin left in a hurry, probably trying to avoid Kydrus's wrath. Had I not been caught in his line of sight, I would have run away, too.

Kydrus spun on his heel and marched down the sidewalk towards his house.

With a sigh, I followed, hanging my head in shame.

Kydrus was one of the Four Warlords. Each warlord presided over a section of Minloa. Usually, with an iron fist. The warlords were the strongest Seelie fae in existence. They ensured the peace was kept, and kept the chaos many fae creatures craved at bay. They gained their titles after the Great War. Our world had been almost decimated, but the four stepped forward and brokered a treaty of peace. That was over one thousand years ago, which was the blink of an eye to the immortals.

Kydrus wore a simple pair of pants and a t-shirt. He had his sword strapped to his side, which ruined his otherwise normal-looking outfit. His dark hair flowed to the middle of his back, the top pulled back just to keep it from falling in his eyes.

His house was in the center of Linta, the main city of the Silpo sector. The three-story, wood and stone house looked as imposing as its owner.

He opened the door and motioned me inside.

Hesitation had me standing at the doorway, my hands gripping the hem of my shirt.

Immortals were patient, and Kydrus had the patience of a saint. He held still, allowing me to work through my issues and ask my question.

"Do you mean to cause me physical harm?" I asked softly.

"No," he answered, his voice as soft as mine had been.

Full-blooded fae could not lie. They could bend the truth and word things in a way that wasn't technically a lie, but his one-word answer gave no room for trickery. So, I entered his house. I had been there several times, and he had yet to harm me, but old wounds caused me to be wary.

Rich earth tones decorated the inside, lots of plush chairs and couches, and his office had a desk made from a dragon's skull. A dragon he had, in fact, killed with his own hands.

I stepped to the side to let him lead the way, keeping my eyes on the wooden floors.

He walked by, his black boots scuffed but clean as they passed.

I followed, my head down like a naughty puppy, and took a seat in one of the chairs situated in front of his desk.

He settled into his chair, his hands clasped in his lap. "What happened this time?"

"Nothing important," I whispered.

"This was the third fight this week."

"They challenged me."

He sighed.

"Kydrus, I—"

My throat closed up. I had been debating showing him my new powers for a week, but feared his reaction. Since he was the one who kept the peace, he would decide if I was too much of a risk, and if I should live or die.

"You can tell me anything, Elara." His voice was soft, coaxing.

My hands clenched into fists in my lap.

I raised my head, met his eyes, and said, "I'm sorry for causing you trouble." That was true. I would tell him about my power some other time.

He smiled, and my heart stuttered. Such a perfect man shouldn't exist. It ought to be against the law to be so handsome, strong, and powerful.

"You're not trouble, Elara. I just want you to stop getting into so many fights."

"I'll try not to get in any more," I said and swallowed past the sudden lump in my throat.

He walked around the desk, and I held still, trying to quell my shaking. Once he was at my side, he reached towards me, and despite my best attempt, I flinched. His hand stilled.

"I'd like to heal you," he whispered. "Unless you enjoy bleeding on everything?"

Taking a deep breath, I nodded.

He set his hand on my shoulder, and his magic flowed into me, speeding my healing.

"Someday, when you are up for it, I would like you to tell me what happened before you came here. Okay?"

"Someday," I agreed.

He removed his hand, and I felt better than normal.

"Thank you."

"You sure there's nothing else you would like to discuss?" he asked softly.

"Not today," I replied, avoiding eye contact.

He nodded and took two steps away from me. "My door is always open to you."

"Thank you."

Sensing my dismissal, I left his home, and walked across town to the small dwelling I called my own. But, as I stood before my empty home, I had no desire to enter. My house was nestled amongst the trees, giving me a break from the craziness of the town. There were two others who lived nearby, but they preferred solitude like me.

Only...I didn't really prefer solitude. I wanted a house full of warmth and love. Or, at least a house full of warmth and friendship. Most of my life I had lived alone. I feared I always would.

Instead of going inside, I headed towards the falls. Very few ventured so far, since it marked the edge of our sector, which was part of the reason I preferred the location. I had never been one to do as the others did.

I walked between the trees, trees that were thousands of years old, reveling in the power they contained. Life magic was very restricted, but we could all sense it. Every living thing contained magic. Using life magic was considered black magic, something the Unseelie used. I was sure to keep my magic tightly coiled when waking in this forest.

The roar of water grew louder as I approached the falls. I walked to the rock outcropping that served as my hide away, and sat with my legs folded beneath me.

From here, I could see the beautiful waterfall, the river it splashed into below, and watch animals come down the hill on the other side to drink water.

Just last week, I had seen a stag and his mate with a fawn. Their coats had been white and their antlers blue.

Most of the time, I was alone with the flowing water.

"I hoped I would find you here, alone," Quin said behind me.

I spun around, on my feet before I thought to do it. "What do you want?" I asked, all too aware that I was dangerously close to the edge.

He snarled, "Your death."

I prepared for his attack, but it didn't matter. He shoved me off the edge, and I screamed as I fell.

A moment before I hit the water, I had the sense to take a breath and hold it. Hitting the water hurt, as did the sting of the ice-cold temperature.

I kicked to the surface, and immediately slammed into a boulder. I cried out in pain.

"Elara!" Kydrus yelled from far away.

"Kyd—"

My word broke off as a tree branch slammed into me. The world went dark.

Someone pounded on my chest, waking me.

I rolled onto my side and vomited water.

Warm hands pressed against my back, keeping me steady.

I lay on the shore, but the landscape looked nothing like home. Golden fields stretched to each side, with flowers of a startling blue color.

"Good. You're alive," an unfamiliar male voice said beside me.

I sat up, and turned to see the speaker. My jaw dropped. A gorgeous man stood before me, shirtless. His silver hair complimented his tanned skin, and I could count every muscle on his ripped body if I had enough time. The muscles on his hips that formed a "V" looked especially delicious.

"Uh, thanks," I said once I got my brain under control and stopped ogling him, bringing my gaze to his.

"What happened to you?" he asked, his brow furrowed.

"Someone shoved me off a cliff," I muttered, rubbing my shoulder. I realized with a start that I didn't have any wounds. "You healed me?"

He nodded.

I looked around us again. "Where are we?"

"Memna," he answered.

Memna was in another sector, ruled by a different warlord than Kydrus. I couldn't remember his name, though.

My eyes widened. "Crap."

"Where are you from?" he asked.

"Silpo. Linta specifically." I ran my fingers through my hair, but it caught on several knots.

His eyes widened. "You're far from home."

Home. That word didn't really mean much to me.

"I can't believe I floated so far downriver," I whispered.

"Well, come on," he said and stood.

"Huh?"

He smirked. "You need some food and rest. I'll take you home with me, and when you're ready to leave, you can."

"Why help me?" I asked, standing and reaching for my sword, but it wasn't there.

He held out my sword. "I mean you no harm. I'm warlord here."

I had been reaching to snatch my sword out of his hands, but that statement stopped me cold in my tracks. "W-warlord?"

He nodded. "I'm Durlan."

Crap. He really was the warlord.

I stepped back and bowed. "I-I'm s-sorry."

"What is your name?"

"Elara."

"As long as you pose no threat to me or my sector, I will not harm you, Elara."

"How far is it to travel back to Linta?" I asked.

"A month's travel by foot," he answered. "Come, it's going to get hot soon, and I'd like to be inside before lunch."

I obeyed, walking behind him with my head bowed. I'd been unconscious through the night. How I hadn't drowned was a miracle.

"Your sword," he said softly, and held it out to me.

I took it, and strapped it to my hip. "Thank you."

"You were a slave?" he asked.

I flinched. Not even Kydrus had guessed.

"Kydrus does not know. If you speak to him, please do not mention it," I whispered.

"Why haven't you told him?" he asked, stopping to face me.

"I do not want him to pity me or view me differently," I answered.

"I will not tell him. It is your story, but I do not think he would pity you. He may view you differently, but not in the way you think. Kydrus is one of the kinder souls in the world."

"I'll think about it." I chewed on my lip.

He nodded and resumed walking. "How long have you been free?"

"Ten years."

He stopped again to face me. "How old are you?"

"Twenty-eight, I think." I didn't really remember the years before I was a slave.

"You escaped?"

I nodded, trying to push away the memories of that awful day.

"Elara, why did someone push you off the cliff?"

I exhaled. "I don't get along well with most of the people in Linta. They like to challenge me to fights, since they know I can't win. I still accept the challenges, though. Kydrus has started breaking them up, before they hurt me too much. It angers them. Quin had hoped to kill me, but his plan failed."

"Do you wish to return to Linta?" he asked, turning to walk backwards so he could look at me.

"What?"

"You do not have to return to Linta. You may stay here, if you wish," he offered.

"I have no home. No real skills. I would be a burden."

"What did you do in Linta?"

"Gathered herbs for one of the potion makers."

He lifted a brow. "What magic do you have?"

My lips pressed together in a tight line, fear worming its way into my blood. I couldn't tell him.

His head dropped forward, and he turned around. "Let's go. We can talk more later."

I followed him into the fields of golden grass, running my hands through it. Should I stay? It might be better than Linta. Though, I would miss some things about Linta, like its warlord.

CHAPTER 2

ELARA

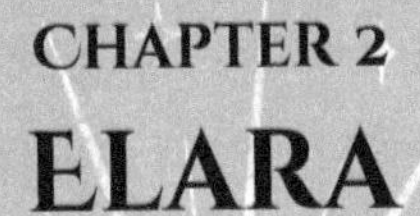

DURLAN TOOK me down a small trail that led to a wide road, and then to a large city.

The city had at least twice as many people as Linta, and the buildings were made of concrete, which gave it a more modern feel.

People placed their hands in fists over their hearts in a sign of respect for Durlan as he passed. He smiled at them, and we walked down the street with no one stopping us.

Many looked at me, but none spoke.

Durlan stopped before an exact replica of Kydrus' house and opened the door.

"Do all the warlords have the same house?" I asked.

He chuckled. "Yes. We had them built at the same time."

Inside, his house was decorated differently than Kydrus's. Instead of earth tones, his house was decorated in bright tones, reminiscent of spring. He also had a dragon skull desk, but his was smaller.

"This way," he called to me, disappearing down the hallway.

I hurried after him, worried, because I had walked straight into his office on habit. “I’m sorry,” I called after him. “Whenever I go to Kydrus’s, it’s to go in his office.”

He chuckled. “So, you’re a troublemaker.”

“No,” I said immediately.

He chuckled again.

I liked his laugh. Kydrus didn’t laugh much.

“What do you like to eat?” he asked.

I followed his voice into the kitchen. “I’ll eat whatever you offer me.”

He was bent over the icebox, looking inside it. He glanced up at me. “Do you live alone in Linta?”

I nodded, my gaze dropping to the ground.

He mumbled something, that included Kydrus’s name, but I couldn’t make it out.

“Take a seat on a stool,” he said. “I’ll make us some lunch.”

There were three stools in front of the kitchen island that I hadn’t seen before. I obeyed, sitting on the stool on the right.

Durlan took out several items from the ice box, as well as from his pantry. I watched with growing confusion and interest as he cut items, put them in a pot or pan, and cooked them.

What was he making?

“Have you never seen someone cook before?” he asked as he stirred the items sizzling in the pan that rested on the stove above flames.

I shook my head.

“What do you usually eat?”

“Roasted rabbit or fruit.”

“You don’t eat during the festivals?”

I met his curious eyes and said, “I’ve never attended one.”

His eyes widened. “How long have you lived with Kydrus?”

“I don’t live—”

“In Linta,” he amended.

“Almost seven years.”

"Why haven't you gone to any?"

I lowered my eyes to the pan, my hands toying with the hem of my shirt. It was still a bit damp, but I didn't want to complain. "I don't like being around large crowds."

He dished out the food into two bowls and slid one to me.

It looked like soup, but there were more vegetables and meat than I was used to. Not soup...stew. I ate it, savoring the various flavors and the combined taste that was unlike anything I had eaten before. Once done, I took my bowl to the sink, cleaned it, and bowed to Durlan who had stayed standing on the opposite side of the island to eat. "Thank you for the meal."

"You don't need to bow to me, Elara."

I gnawed on my bottom lip and nodded.

"Do you bow to Kydrus?"

"Not anymore," I answered.

He chuckled. "Well, you don't need to bow to me either." He patted my stool, but then he scowled and looked at his hand. "Your clothes are still wet?"

"Sorry. I'll get a towel—"

He stood. "Come with me."

Fear consumed me. He seemed nice, but would he hurt me because I had gotten his stool wet? One would hope the warlords weren't so easily angered, but they were very old.

I obediently followed him, surprised when he led me to the bathroom.

"Why don't you take a shower or bath? I'll get you some clean clothes," he said and turned on the water.

He left before I could say anything.

Quickly, I stripped and stepped into the shower. The floor was recessed and there was a plug to turn it into a bathtub, but I preferred showers. It was much safer to be in showers.

"Here's your cloth—" Durlan said, then stopped.

I looked over my shoulder at him. "Thank you."

He walked to me, a scowl pulling his brows together, and a snarl pulling up his lips.

I froze. "D-did I do something wrong?"

He reached out and touched one of my many scars. "What are these from?"

"Whips," I answered, my heart beating faster than a hummingbird flapped their tiny wings.

He traced his fingertip along one, the puckered flesh still red despite it being over a decade old.

I shivered. No one had touched my scars before.

He raised his eyes to meet mine. "Where were you a slave?"

I couldn't tell him. If I did, I would be hunted.

"Who was your master?"

I shook my head as tears fell down my cheeks, mixing with the shower water.

"I won't hurt you. I must know what sector you were a slave in. Just tell me that."

"Tresca," I answered, my body began to shake despite the warm water falling down my body.

He rested his hand on my back a moment, closed his eyes, and before I could ask what he was doing, he shoved power into my scars.

I gasped and would have fallen had he not wrapped an arm around my waist and held me up.

Memories of my whippings and time as a slave flashed before me, as did memories of many of my fights in Linta. And then, it stopped.

I opened my eyes, surprised to find that I was sitting in Durlan's lap on the floor of the shower with the water falling on both of us.

My head lay against his chest, while he stroked my hair.

"Wh-what was that?" I asked with a hoarse voice.

Had I been screaming?

"I'm sorry. I won't do that again. But I had to see."

See?

My eyes widened. He had used magic to pull the memories from my scars. I had heard of a power like that but didn't realize it belonged to one of the warlords.

"Kydrus has never seen your back, has he?"

I shook my head. I should have probably stood and moved away from him, but he made me feel safe. It was nice to be held.

"Finish your shower and then meet me in my office," he ordered me as he stood, lifting me to my feet as he did.

Once he shut the door, I slumped back to the floor with my head in my hands. How could everything go so wrong in just two days?

I didn't want to keep Durlan waiting, so I quickly cleaned myself and dressed in the clothes he had provided. They were soft and smelled like him.

I stood in the doorway to his office, gnawing on my lip.

What would he do? I hadn't actually told him anything, so it wasn't my fault he had discovered who my owner had been.

"Come, sit by me, please," he said softly.

I looked up, and my brows immediately furrowed. He had placed a chair beside his, while three more sat in front of his desk. Who was he inviting over?

I sat in the chair he had indicated, and he smiled at me.

"They'll be here shortly."

"Who?" I asked.

"Elara!" Kydrus boomed as he entered the room.

I leapt to my feet. How had he gotten here so fast?

Kydrus strode forward, looking like he meant to touch me, but Durlan stepped into his path.

Kydrus scowled. "Durlan, step aside."

He shook his head. "You're scaring her."

He was, but how had Durlan known?

Kydrus's shoulders drooped, and he looked around Durlan at me. "I'm glad you're safe. I executed Quin, so you won't have to worry about him anymore."

Executed?

Kydrus smiled. "Did you think I would let him live after he tried to kill you?"

Yes.

"Sit," Durlan ordered him. He turned to me. "Kydrus won't hurt you. You're under my protection now, so no one will hurt you. Understand?"

No.

I nodded and sat back in my chair.

Kydrus sat as well. "What happened?" he asked me.

"Quin pushed me off the ledge, and I fell in the river. I woke up on the shore, here, with Durlan saving me," I answered.

"Why summon us all?" Kydrus asked.

"Patience," Durlan said with a smile and sat beside me again.

Two more males entered, and I knew they were the other two warlords without being told. Both were just as muscular as Kydrus and Durlan, but these two had short hair, cut close to their ears.

They stopped their whispering when they saw me.

The one on the right had magenta eyes, and three scars down his left cheek. He smiled. "Did you take a mate?"

I tensed. Mate? No, he wouldn't force me to be his mate, would he?

Kydrus scoffed. "She is *not* his mate."

The fourth male had massive shoulders, crystal blue eyes, and a scowl. "She looks familiar."

"Sit," Durlan said with a sigh.

They took the two remaining seats in front of the desk.

"I've brought you all here because one of us has broken the treaty," Durlan said.

Oh no!

"What?" the scarred man asked.

"Who?" Kydrus asked, his hand going to the hilt of his sword.

"How?" the warlord on the right demanded.

I flinched at their shouts, and Durlan set his hand on top of mine. His hand was warm and calloused. It also helped me relax.

"Venali, were you aware you have slaves in your sector?"

The man on the right turned towards the scarred man, while Kydrus looked at me with wide eyes.

Venali, the brute with the scars, asked, "What have you heard? I've no knowledge of slaves in my sector. I have no knowledge of slaves anywhere in Minloa."

They couldn't lie, and his statement let me relax. At least he wasn't involved.

"Elara," Durlan said softly and squeezed my hand.

I looked up at him, feeling like a child.

"Will you show them your scars?" he asked softly.

Kydrus tensed. "Scars?"

I swallowed, nodded, and stood, pulling off my shirt as I did, and turned my back to them. I clutched the shirt to my chest to hide my breasts.

Two of them, I wasn't certain which two, sucked in a breath between their teeth.

I turned, and dropped my hands, letting them see the scars on my chest and stomach as well.

Durlan's eyes widened. "You didn't show me those."

I shrugged. "You didn't ask to see the rest."

I started to pull off my pants, but Durlan stopped me. "That's alright. They've seen enough. You can put your shirt back on."

I obeyed, dressed, and sat, avoiding the gazes of the other men.

"You're certain it is my sector?" Venali asked.

Durlan picked up an orb from the shelf behind his desk, and then began replaying the memories he had taken from my scars.

I squeezed my eyes closed and tried to ignore the sounds of the whip, but flinched with each one. My teeth ground together, and tears threatened to fall.

"She was a child," the fourth warlord said. Since the other was Venali, that meant he was Amrynn, Warlord of the Blustum sector.

Venali hadn't spoken since viewing the memories.

Neither had Kydrus.

Durlan set his hand on mine again, squeezing gently.

I glanced up at him, and he slowly reached over to wipe my face. I hadn't realized that the tears had fallen.

"She never told me what happened before she came to Linta," Kydrus said softly. "I had my suspicions, but I didn't want to believe them. I also had no idea how badly the others were treating her."

Durlan nodded. "She told me."

I saw Kydrus's hands clenched into fists in his lap.

"I did not know about the slavery," Venali said finally. "I will end it once I return."

"Her owner?" Kydrus asked.

"He will be brought before us for punishment. To make an example of him," Venali said, his voice a growl. "Girl," he said softly.

"Elara," Kydrus and Durlan said at the same time.

"Elara," Venali said.

I looked at him. He looked pained. Why?

"Did they do more than beat you?" he asked softly.

Oh. That's why he looked pained.

"No."

All four males let out a breath.

"How did you escape?" Kydrus asked.

I stood and set my sword on the desk. "This belonged to his son. I took it. They didn't know I had been watching them and practicing with twigs."

"You killed them?" Durlan asked, shock coloring his tone.

I smirked. "No. I took an arm from each of them."

Venali reached for the sword, and I snatched it back.

"It's mine! I earned it," I growled.

Venali and Amrynn smiled at me, which was a strange reaction to a woman growling at them.

"I will not keep your battle treasure," Venali said gently. "I just want to touch it to identify the owners."

Now that I realized what I had done, I dropped it and sat down in my chair with my hands beneath my legs.

What was wrong with me? I had just snapped at a warlord.

Venali touched the hilt and closed his eyes. The sword began to glow blue, and then it returned to normal and he removed his hand. He nodded. "I know who they are."

"Were there other slaves?" Durlan asked me.

I nodded. "He sold most of them to another male. Only me and two others stayed with him."

Venali scowled. "Another?"

"At least two others, actually," I said as I thought back. "There might have been more."

"Would you like my assistance?" Amrynn asked Venali.

Venali nodded, his scowl still in place.

"Two weeks?" Durlan asked.

Venali nodded again. "That should be sufficient time for me to capture them."

"There's something else," Durlan said.

All eyes turned to him, including mine.

What else could there be?

Durlan turned to face me. "At sundown, you will show us your powers."

I gulped.

"What is the meaning of this?" Kydrus asked.

"She has hidden her powers from you," Durlan said, still looking at me.

How did he know? I hadn't told him what my powers were. Had he seen something when he'd touched my scars?

"Elara?" Kydrus questioned, his voice soft.

I swallowed again. "I was going to tell you...last night. But..."

"But what?" Kydrus prompted.

I met his eyes and said, "I was afraid you would kill me."

The tension in the room skyrocketed.

I resigned myself to my fate. I might be able to run from one warlord, but I didn't stand a chance with all four of them here. I lowered my eyes to my lap.

"Why not just tell us what the power is?" Venali asked.

"Because it must be witnessed," Durlan said. "She's quite glorious."

Glorious?

I looked at him, and he was smiling down at me.

"Am I allowed to hold my sword?" I asked.

He nodded. "It is yours."

I took it slowly and secured it to my side.

"Can I speak to her alone?" Kydrus asked.

"No," Durlan said immediately, before my fear could even register.

"I have no desire to harm her," Kydrus grumbled.

"You scare her," Durlan said. "She's been traumatized enough."

Fidgeting in my chair, I kept my eyes down to avoid meeting Kydrus's gaze, which I could feel piercing me.

"Elara will stay here until sundown. The rest of us will discuss other matters in the kitchen," Durlan ordered everyone.

I thought the warlords were equal, but he seemed to be ordering everyone around, and they were listening. Was there a pecking order even amongst the warlords?

Venali, Amrynn, and Kydrus left the room.

Durlan knelt by my chair. "Will you be alright in here alone?"

I nodded. "Yes, sir."

He set his hand on mine, and I looked up to find him smiling. "You can call me Durlan. I'll come bring you dinner when it's ready."

I nodded and watched him leave with a sense of foreboding. Either I died tonight, or my life was going to change. How? I didn't know, and that scared me almost as much as death.

CHAPTER 3
DURLAN

THE THINGS that Elara had dealt with in her short life appalled me.

For someone so young to have been beaten and enslaved, enraged me to the point of wanting to find the man myself and tear his head off. I wasn't normally one for violence first, but the ones who had hurt her deserved nothing less than death.

"What is special about her?" Amrynn asked, looking at me. "She feels..."

"You have to wait to see her magic," I answered with a smug smile. Their reactions were going to be priceless.

"You know?" Kydrus asked.

I met his eyes. "You don't?"

He scowled. "If I knew, I wouldn't be asking."

"This is turning out to be an amazing day," I chuckled. "I find a beautiful girl in the river, save her life, find out something none of you know, and get to watch your faces when she shows you who she really is."

"Just tell us," Venali growled.

I shook my head. "Not a chance. The last time I was able to surprise one of you was decades ago. I'm going to savor this."

"Are we going to have to kill her?" Venali asked softly.

I could hear the hesitancy in his voice, which surprised me.

She was magnetic, and her fear spoke to our animalistic urges to protect her. It helped that she was attractive, but I would have felt the same even if she hadn't been.

Venali was normally one to kill first and worry about the repercussions later. Was he hesitant because he felt partially responsible for her enslavement in his sector? Or was it her blood, which called to me, too? It appeared she didn't even know her bloodlines and the true power she possessed.

"No," I answered Venali. "In fact, you're going to want to be near her as often as possible."

"Why are you keeping me from her? I've been interacting with her for years before you were involved," Kydrus growled.

"You frighten her. She admitted she thought you were going to kill her when you discovered her magic. Plus, after seeing what she went through as a child, how can you not understand that she'd be hesitant for a man to touch her when he is upset?"

He grumbled under his breath in response.

"Let's make food, gentlemen. Then, when the sun sets, that terrified woman will forever change our lives."

And, I could not wait.

CHAPTER 4
ELARA

Durlan had delivered my dinner, and then he had left me to eat alone.

I was used to eating alone, but knowing they were together in the other room made me feel even more alone than usual. I felt like I was eating my final supper. The food tasted like dust, my heart pounding faster with each bite.

The sun set, and my heart pounded furiously in my chest while my hands sweated. The uncertainty of their responses to my magic was the worst. I rubbed my hands on my pants, trying to get them to stop sweating.

Durlan didn't seem worried or upset about my powers, but that didn't mean the others would share his opinion.

Durlan opened the door, smiling. "It's time."

I stood on shaky legs and walked to him.

"Do you need anything?" he asked.

"A bottle or jar with a lid?"

He smirked. "Are you asking or telling?"

"Both," I whispered, looking down at his boots.

He fetched me one, and then escorted me outside to the back of his house where a field of flowers swayed in the breeze.

Venali, Kydrus, and Amrynn stood side by side, waiting expectantly.

Durlan set the jar on the ground with the lid open, then walked to stand beside the other warlords, but I noticed he was turned so he could look at them at the same time as me.

This was it. The moment I would find out if they were going to kill me or not. I would use my magic, and then they would smite me or...I wasn't sure what they would do.

I met all of their gazes a moment, and then lifted my head to the stars. I stretched out my arms, let the light of the stars and planets fill me, making my body glow. I crouched, picked up the jar, and raised my hand to gently grab one of the stars. Carefully, I pulled it from the sky and put it in the jar. I closed the lid, secured the clasp, and held it out towards them. The light still illuminated my body, but it was a soft glow now, slowly fading.

None of them moved. It didn't even look like they were breathing.

I took a few tentative steps closer to them, set the jar on the ground just in front of their feet, and then hurried backwards, clutching the hilt of my sword.

Durlan squatted down and looked at the star and started to reach for the clasp.

"No!" I yelled.

He stilled, looking up at me.

"I can release it, but if you do that, it will just come out full sized, right here," I explained.

"She plucked a star from the sky," Venali whispered. Was that awe I heard in his voice?

"If it came out, could you shrink it again?" Durlan asked.

I nodded.

"It was you," Kydrus gasped. "The crater by the lake."

I flinched and nodded. I had tried to forget that day.

"She's her. It's her!" Amrynn moved towards me quickly, his mouth agape.

I drew my sword and backed up. The sword shook as I held it out in front of me, trying to keep him at bay.

He stopped walking and held out his hands. "Elara, do you remember your life before you were sold as a slave?"

I shook my head.

He smiled. "You're a princess. Well, queen now. You are *our* queen."

"We don't have a monarchy," I reminded him.

"We used to," he said and cocked his head to the side. "Was she frozen or something? She should be a lot older."

"We need to find Azael," Venali said.

Azael had been my owner. Why did he want to find him? Aside from him having been a slave owner, that is.

I lowered my sword. "So, you're not going to kill me?"

Amrynn walked forward slowly and dropped to one knee, his head bowed to me. "Quite the opposite. Queen Elara, I pledge myself as your guard and vow to give my life for yours, should the need arise."

This was a joke, right? He had to be joking.

"I'm not a queen. I am...I was a slave. I am nothing," I said, backing away from him.

"You are everything," Durlan said as he walked closer. He bowed on one knee beside Amrynn.

Venali broke from his stupor and came to a knee beside the other two.

This was insanity.

Kydrus still stood in the same place, staring at me.

"Kydrus, what do I do?" I asked him softly. "I don't understand what's going on. This is crazy."

He blinked a few times. Then, he walked to the others and

knelt beside them. "You let us help you. You let us protect you, my queen."

THE FOUR WARLORDS ESCORTED ME BACK INTO THE HOUSE.

Durlan took the jar with the star in it and set it on his desk. He promised to seal it so no one would accidentally unleash the star.

"First, we need to find the one who owned her, question him extensively, and try to find out what happened," Venali said.

The other three nodded.

"If I'm the queen, that means my parents were royalty as well."

My mind was still reeling from their proclamations and I felt that they had to be wrong.

All four turned to face me.

"They were murdered before the Great War," I continued. "I can't be that old."

"The only explanation would be that you were frozen or in a state of suspended animation," Amrynn said. "You went missing as a child, the night before your parents were killed, actually. Maybe they knew and sent you away."

"How could I have been frozen?" Or survived being frozen? People didn't just get frozen all the time. It wasn't a normal occurrence.

"There are a few who could have performed the spell," Kydrus said.

"This is insane," I whispered and walked to sit in front of the fireplace. I didn't want to be a queen. I just wanted to be free to do as I liked.

"We can't all stay in one place," Durlan said. "Our sectors will destabilize if we aren't there."

Kydrus sighed. "You're right, but what should we do?"

"What if we set up a rotation?" Amrynn suggested. "She could stay with each of us for one month at a time."

"One month?" Kydrus asked. "Why not two weeks?"

"It's not fair for us to make her move around that often. I'd rather it be once every three months," Durlan said.

"Once a month is a decent compromise," Venali commented.

I swiveled on my butt to face them. All four sat in chairs now, Durlan in his desk chair.

"Are you talking about me?" I asked.

Durlan nodded.

"We are discussing where you'll be staying and for how long," Kydrus explained.

"Why do I have to move around? Can't I just stay in one place?"

Moving always made me anxious. Being in a new place was always unnerving.

"Where would you stay?" Kydrus asked. He glanced sideways at Durlan before looking back to me. "You have a preferred place?"

"You need to be with one of us at all times," Amrynn said. "There are some who will not like the idea of having a monarch again."

"Maybe we shouldn't have a monarch," I said softly. "If they were so unhappy that they murdered my parents, they'll likely come for me, too."

"They will come for you. That's why you need to be protected," Kydrus said quickly, his brows furrowed.

"If we don't tell them who I am, and I return to a normal life, they won't know to come for me," I argued.

"They'll know," Kydrus replied.

"How? I lived in your city for almost a decade, saw you almost every single day, and you didn't know who I was," I snapped.

His expression tightened, and I immediately regretted my outburst.

"I sensed it as soon as I saw you," Durlan said. "I thought I was wrong, but the longer I was with you, the more I felt it."

"Felt what?" My brows furrowed, and I tried to sense anything different in myself.

"Cosmic power," Amrynn said with awe in his voice and admiration in his eyes. "We could tell you were different, we just weren't sure how."

"I don't want to be a queen. There's no reason to change our society. You four have been ruling and there have been no wars. Why change it?" I looked at each one in turn, trying to ensure they agreed.

All four were unconvinced.

"She will stay with me first," Durlan told them. "Amrynn next, then Venali, and then Kydrus. Then, we will repeat the cycle."

"This is ridiculous," I grumbled and left the office. I walked out to the grassy field and lay on my back, looking up at the stars.

Why wouldn't they listen to reason? I knew nothing of ruling. I could barely read!

Amyrnn lay on his back beside me, his hands beneath his head.

I waited for him to speak, but he didn't.

"Why don't you four have mates?" I asked while still staring up at the stars.

"I don't know about the others, but for me, none were ever the right one for me," he said. "Many were beautiful, but our personalities didn't mesh. Some had good personalities, but they just didn't feel right. I want a partner. I want someone who fits beside me and feels like my missing piece. Like their presence fills and completes me."

"That's a pretty tall order," I muttered.

He chuckled. "I suppose it is."

I turned my head to look at him. "What if you never find someone who meets those requirements?"

He smiled. "She's out there. I just haven't found her yet."

"I hope you find her," I whispered. He was so old already. Would he go his entire life being alone?

"What about you, Elara?" he asked.

"Me?" I asked, eyes widened.

He nodded. "You're beautiful. Why don't you have a mate?"

I wanted a mate. I wanted someone who would love me and only me for the rest of our lives.

"Because she hides from everyone," Kydrus answered.

I raised my head.

Kydrus walked towards us, scowling.

"I wondered when you would stop hiding in the shadows," Amyrnn whispered with a smirk.

"I don't have a mate because no man has approached me." I lay back down and looked at the stars. "I'm too different than them. My beauty pales next to my weirdness, I guess."

Both men chuckled.

I sat up to face them. "What?"

"I need to go," Kydrus said, ignoring my question. "I'll see you in a few months."

Amrynn stood and brushed himself off. "I should go as well." He held out his hand, and I set mine in it. With a quick pull, he had me on my feet and wrapped in a hug. He was warm and solid muscle. Being hugged by him was incredible. "I'll see you in a month," he whispered in my ear. "Stay safe, my queen."

He released me and disappeared.

"Can I walk you back to the house before I leave?" Kydrus asked.

"Sure," I replied, my cheeks warm from Amrynn's embrace.

Kydrus walked by my side until we got to the back door of Durlan's house. He leaned forward and hugged me quickly. Then he stepped back and disappeared. Had that been a pained expression on his face?

Was he upset that I was royalty? Did it pain him to know that I, the pathetic girl who caused so many problems for him, was a queen?

"There you are," Venali said, startling me out of my inner thoughts.

"You were looking for me?" I asked, looking up at him. I wanted to trace his scars with my fingertips but clenched my hands into fists to keep from doing so.

He stepped forward, closing the distance between us. "I have to leave. I'll see you in two months, okay?"

Of the four, he made me feel the safest. Like I knew he would kill anything that tried to hurt me. There was zero logical reasoning for this, and yet that was how I felt.

I nodded.

He bent a placed a kiss on my cheek. "Be safe."

"You, too," I whispered, my throat suddenly tight.

He smiled, and then he too disappeared.

"You look exhausted," Durlan said from the doorway.

"Does a pixie bite?" I scoffed. "I'm just in need of a long rest."

"Let me show you to your room," he said and held open the door.

"Durlan, why are you all so adamant that I become queen?" I asked as I followed him to one of the spare rooms.

He stepped into the room and leaned against the wall beside the door. "We prosper best when we have a strong matriarch."

"Are you four just tired of ruling?" I asked, leaning my hip against the dresser. Everything was in pristine condition, there wasn't even dust on the furniture. Was he a neat freak?

He smiled. "Even when you take over as queen, we will still be your warlords, and in charge of our sectors."

"Why do I have to be passed around every month? Why can't I

find a place at the point all of the sectors meet and build a place there?"

"You don't want to stay with the others? Are you scared of them?"

"It has nothing to do with them," I said. And no, I wasn't scared of them. I probably should have been. "Why not just pick some guards for me and let me live in the middle?"

He scowled. "You want to find random men to guard you?"

"I would let you four pick them, so we knew they were trustworthy."

"Are we unappealing to you?" he asked.

"Your appeal has nothing to do with this," I grumbled.

He smirked. "So, you do find us appealing."

"Do I look blind?" I asked and scoffed.

He laughed and the sound made me smile.

"What does a queen even do?"

"That's part of why we will have you take turns staying with us. Each of us excels in different knowledge bases. For example, I'm the best strategist. Venalis is our best fighter, and so on."

"I didn't realize Venali was a better fighter. I thought you were all fairly equal."

He smirked again. "Do not misunderstand, we can all hold our own, but in a battle, Venali always gets the highest kill count."

"Did you bring the other two here when confronting Venali about my slavery in case he did know and attacked you?"

He nodded.

I exhaled and ran a hand through my hair. "I'm glad that wasn't the case."

"You and me both," Durlan said with a chuckle. "I didn't truly believe he knew, but I take whatever precautions I need to."

"Durlan, I..." I felt I should let him know my limitations. An illiterate queen would be laughed at.

He walked to me and set his hands on my upper arms with a smile. "You can tell me anything, Elara."

"I can't read," I blurted.

He nodded. "Kydrus told us."

My mouth dropped open. "How did he know?'

He smiled. "He may not have consciously known who you were, but he always felt something with you. Didn't you find it odd that he kept interrupting your fights?"

I had, but I figured it had been because of my obvious fear. And, because they kept picking on me.

"Do I have to stay in Linta for a month?" I asked softly, letting my head drop forward.

"You don't want to be with Kydrus?"

My cheeks warmed. "It has nothing to do with him. I just don't like Linta."

"You should get to know each of us, the warlords, and our sectors."

I looked up at him. "Get to know you? Why?"

He smiled again. "Because we are your warlords."

The way he said it made it clear he was hiding something. The fluttering in my chest meant I wasn't sure if it was good or bad.

He stepped back from me, dropping his hands from my arms. "You should sleep. Tomorrow, I begin your tutoring." He closed my bedroom door after a quick, "Good night, my queen."

CHAPTER 5
KYDRUS

Elara was our lost princess. How had I not seen that before? I'd felt a connection to her. I'd felt that there was something different about her, but I never would have imagined this.

The urge to protect her had been impossible to ignore the longer I was around her, which was why I had kept stopping her fights. But knowing who she was now, I wanted to resurrect Quin and kill him all over again.

She had suffered so much in her short life, and she should have never endured any of it. Had her parents not sent her away, she would have been protected, and none of this would have happened. None of those scars would mar her body. Not that it took away from her beauty. If anything, it made her even more beautiful, to have endured so much and still have so much love.

Or, had she stayed with her parents, she might have met the same fate as them. I wished to go back in time and take her to safety myself.

Her former owner would pay. I would kill him slowly.

And somehow, I would make her understand that I would never harm her.

CHAPTER 6
ELARA

Tutoring was clearly a synonym for torture.

"Can we please take a break?" I begged Durlan.

We had spent the past three hours going over the history of Minloa, but hadn't made it to the Great War yet.

He chuckled. "Alright, we can break for lunch."

I doubted I had ever smiled wider in my life.

Durlan wore jeans and a t-shirt with dusty boots. He didn't carry a sword like Kydrus did, and when I had asked why, he said, "I don't have much need for it."

Durlan took out some ingredients, and then waved me over. I sat on a stool at the island, and folded my arms on the top.

"Do you want to learn to cook?" he asked.

"Yes," I said eagerly.

"First, we need to cut up these vegetables." He cut one of the vegetables with a large knife into small slices to show me, and then he slid the cutting board, knife, and other vegetables to me. "Now, you try."

I moved slowly, but my cuts were never the same size.

"Elara," Venali said loudly behind me.

I jumped, cut my finger with the knife, and hissed in pain. The wound immediately began bleeding.

Durlan reached across the table for my hand, but Venali beat him to it.

Venali cradled my bleeding hand in his giant palm and used his magic to heal me. "I'm sorry," he said softly. "I didn't mean to startle you."

"It's okay," I said. "It was just a small cut."

"I just came to let you know that I found Azael. And, he admitted everything," Venali continued.

"Did he say how he found her?" Durlan asked.

Venali finished healing me and took a damp cloth and cleaned the blood off my hand. For such a large and dangerous man, he was surprisingly gentle.

"He did. I'd like to show you something," he told Durlan.

Durlan glanced at me. "She'll have to come."

"I can just stay here, if you don't want me going."

Venali shook his head and met my eyes. "It's your past. You should come, too."

Staring into his eyes, I became very aware of how close he stood to me, the fact that he was still holding my hand, and that his leg was touching mine. His eyes swirled with emotions too fast for me to pinpoint one.

Durlan cleared his throat, and Venali moved away so fast that I thought I'd somehow hurt him.

"We were about to eat. Can it wait?" Durlan asked.

Venali nodded. "I actually haven't eaten yet. Do you have enough for me?"

"Yes," Durlan said.

I stood, grabbed a towel, got it wet, and then began cleaning the island, trying to get all of my blood off of it

Venali washed the knife and cutting board, threw away the pieces of vegetable my blood contaminated, and then with a speed and skill I doubted I would ever have, sliced the rest up in perfectly identical pieces.

He caught me staring, arched an eyebrow, and asked, "What?"

"Just impressed," I said softly.

He chuckled. "If that impresses you, I can't wait to see what you think when you see me fight."

Durlan whispered something into his ear that made the smile on Venali's face disappear.

"What?" I asked.

"You never ate meals with Kydrus?" Venali asked instead of answering me.

"No. Why would I?" I scowled. Who just ate meals with their warlord?

"Do you dislike Kydrus? Or are you scared of him?" Venali asked.

"I like Kydrus. At times, I was frightened of him. I was worried he would finally grow tired of me and kill me. Or, when he found out about my powers that he would kill me. Only an idiot isn't scared of the Four Warlords."

Both Durlan and Venali were smiling now. Clearly, they liked what I'd said.

"Your smiles worry me," I grumbled and averted my gaze, looking down at my hands.

"I'll finish up lunch. Why don't you go help her sharpen her sword?" Durlan suggested.

Venali said, "Sounds great. Come on, Elara. I'll teach you the proper way to sharpen knives and swords."

I cast a nervous glance at Durlan, but he was already cooking.

"I promise, I won't bite. Unless you bite me first," Venali whispered in my ear. His warm breath caressed my earlobe and made me shiver. I wouldn't mind a few bites from Venali.

I followed him outside to a wooden building I hadn't noticed before. He threw open the huge double doors with ease. When he headed in, I tried tugging on one of the doors. My suspicions were confirmed, each door was heavy, and he'd opened them like normal doors.

Inside were all the equipment and tools a blacksmith would have. Did Durlan make his own weapons?

"Sword," Venali requested.

I drew my sword, set it on my palms, and held it out to him.

He gently took it, raised it, and examined all of its angles. "Have you ever attacked someone with this?"

I nodded.

"Did you cut them?"

I shook my head.

He chuckled. "I didn't think so."

"Why do you say that?"

"It's incredibly blunt. If you'd had to defend yourself against us last night, and tried to stab one of us, we would have been really irritated at getting poked by this."

"I already know I don't stand a chance against you four," I mumbled, heat flooding my cheeks.

"What about one of us? You drew your weapon on Amrynn."

"If you were faced with opponents beyond your skill, but they were going to kill you, would you have drawn your weapon or just accepted your fate?" I asked with an arched brow and hands on my hips.

"We weren't going to kill you," he said softly.

"I didn't know that. And, you didn't answer me."

He smirked. "Yes, I would have drawn my weapon." He looked back at my sword. "It's going to take me a bit to sharpen this. I think our lesson will have to wait until you come see me. I'll sharpen your sword today while you observe."

I sat on a nearby stool so I could watch him. "Thank you."

"What has Durlan been teaching you today?" he asked while he worked.

"History," I said and tried to hide my displeasure.

He chuckled. "It is important to know your history."

"I don't want to be queen," I told him.

He looked up at me. "If I could prevent it, I would, but it is your birthright and destiny."

"Does that mean I'll be forced to mate some pompous man so he can be king?" I asked.

Venali set the sword down to look at me. "What?"

"I don't want to be forced to mate with someone I don't love," I told him.

"You don't have to worry about that," he promised me.

"I don't?"

He smiled. "I'll ensure it doesn't happen."

"How?" I asked skeptically.

"I'll kill anyone who tries to force you to mate with anyone against your will."

I believed him. The fire in his eyes, the power that flared around him, were all signs of his promise.

"Thank you."

He bowed. "I'll do almost anything you ask me to, my queen."

"Could you stop calling me that then?"

He chuckled. "I'll try."

"Will you do me one other favor?" I asked before I lost my nerve.

"What?"

"Teach me to fight."

He smiled so wide, I thought his face might get stuck that way. Not that it was bad. Actually, he was quite handsome when he smiled. "It would be my honor," he said.

We lapsed into silence while he sharpened my sword and then polished it.

When he was done, I could see my reflection in the blade.

He held it out, but before I could reach it, he drew it back.

"Why do you want to learn to fight? I will teach you, but I'd like to know why."

"I don't want to be helpless ever again. I want to be able to protect myself."

"We will protect you," he said adamantly, but his eyes were soft.

"You won't always be with me," I countered.

His head cocked to the side. "He hasn't told you?"

"Told me what?"

"We're your warlords. We are your guards and your assassins."

"You have sectors to keep in line. You can't leave them to guard me."

I remembered Amrynn vowing to be my guard, but I thought it had been metaphorical.

He smiled. "When you are queen, we won't have to rule our sectors. We will stay with you, and if something comes up, one of us will go."

"What if something happens in all four sectors at the same time?"

"Then you'll accompany me," he said.

"Why you?"

He smirked. "Because no one will touch you if I am by your side."

"Cocky much?" I teased.

"No, just honest." He shrugged nonchalantly.

"I suggested you find me guards, but Durlan didn't like that idea," I said softly.

"You would rather have random men guard you, then the Four Warlords?" His eyebrows rose, and he set my sword down on the anvil.

"I would rather find a place in the mountains where I could live in peace, than be queen. I would rather not be a burden. You are each over a thousand years old. I can't imagine you'd want to spend your time entertaining a child."

He scowled. "First, you aren't a burden or a child. Second, we would be protecting our queen. It is a very honorable job. Third, we may be old, but that just means we know what we want and what is fun."

"What do you want?" I asked, looking up at him.

He moved closer and stared down into my eyes. "The better question is, what do *you* want?"

He was so close, so warm, and so powerful. I knew without a doubt he could protect me. I hoped he would be loyal. I dreamed that he would kiss me. I wanted to be in his arms.

I swallowed and whispered, "To be l—"

"Lunch is ready," Durlan said from the doorway.

The spell was broken. I turned and smiled. "Great! I'm starving." I left the two men behind me, and hurried to the house. Instead of going to the kitchen, I went to the bathroom and sat on the floor with my head against the door. What was wrong with me? I had almost told Venali that I wanted to be loved.

I groaned and dropped my face into my hands.

I was a moron.

Hiding in the bathroom wouldn't accomplish anything. I had to face them.

With a deep breath for courage, I went to the kitchen and sat on the open stool between Venali and Durlan. I picked up the fork and ate the food on my plate. I didn't know what it was, but it was tasty.

Neither man said anything while we ate.

Once done, they stood and held out their hands to me.

I looked back and forth, not sure what to do. Was this a test? I didn't know either man well. I didn't have a favorite.

Durlan was nice and smart.

Venali was strong and dangerous.

I grabbed each of their hands, which earned me a smile from both of them.

Venali put my sword in my sheath, and then teleported us to a dark cave. I tensed once we arrived, fear clawing at me. The urge to escape, to run, was so intense that my legs were taut in preparation.

Venali pulled me into a hug, wrapping his strong arms around me. "Breathe, Elara. You are safe. We won't hurt you. And, I won't let anything else hurt you."

Slowly, my heart returned to a more normal rhythm. Or, as normal as it could be with Venali's arms around me.

He released me, but then grabbed my hand in his much larger one and tugged me after him.

This cave felt familiar. There was nothing out of the ordinary about the cave, and yet I felt like I'd been here.

Durlan followed silently behind.

We walked down a narrow tunnel, which was dark and probably filled with bugs. I was very glad I couldn't see them.

Light ahead drew my attention. It glowed like fey lanterns.

We entered the large cave, and my entire body went rigid.

Wooden furniture lay in broken pieces, scattered across the cave, a few books lay discarded on the ground, and what looked like a bed took up one side. What drew the most attention was the white wall with a child-sized hole.

I approached it, my hand raised, but Venali tugged me to a stop before I could.

"I'm not sure what would happen if you touched it," he whispered.

"They froze me here," I whispered. "Then, someone broke me out. They shattered the crystal with an ax," I told them as snippets of my memory returned. I'd been so scared when I'd woken up with unfamiliar men standing around me.

I sank to my knees, clutching my head as all of my memories returned, and I felt whole for the first time ever.

I stood and turned to Venali.

"Who froze you?" Venali asked softly.

"Take me to the castle," I ordered him.

"It was destroyed," Durlan said.

I shook my head. "No, it wasn't. Take me. I'll show you."

"We should bring the others," Durlan told Venali.

Venali nodded. "I'll wait at your house."

We teleported back to Durlan's front yard, and I sank to my knees on the grass.

It was true. I was the princess, now queen. My parents had sent me away.

Venali sat beside me, his brows furrowed. "Are you okay?"

"I remember," I whispered. "I remember that night. I remember my life before I was a slave."

His eyes widened.

Tears dripped down my cheeks. My parents, my loving and wonderful parents, were dead. Murdered. I was glad I hadn't witnessed it, but the stories about it had never affected me before. Now, now it hurt so much.

Venali repositioned himself so that his legs were on either side of me, then pulled me closer, so I sat with my back to his chest. He wrapped his arms around me.

I turned sideways so I basically sat in his lap and hid my face against his shirt.

"I'm sorry. I wasn't a guard back then. I can't imagine how scared you were when they broke you out of your crystal."

"So alone," I whispered, sniffling.

"You're not alone now," he whispered back and stroked my hair. "You'll never be alone again."

"When you find mates, I will be. Unless I've found a mate by then. Which, I doubt."

"We won't take mates," he whispered against my hair. "We want no mate besides—"

"We?"

"The four of us," he explained.

"What about you?" My tears had stopped. I wiped my eyes. "What do you want, Venali?"

"You to live a long and healthy life."

"You don't know me. Just because I have the same bloodlines as someone else doesn't mean you should care."

"You're young and haven't been taught," he said with a sigh.

I stood with a glare at him. "That's not my fault."

He stood, too. "I just meant that you need to learn what we really are to you. What it really means for us to be your warlords."

"Then tell me."

"We are your guards. Your advisors. And, your mates," he said softly.

I blinked. "Mates? I thought you said I wouldn't be forced to mate with someone I don't love?"

"You won't."

I rubbed my temples. "You are not making any sense."

"We are your mates, but you don't have to mate with us. If you choose to only mate with one of us, the other three will still be your warlords. So, really, we are your potential mates. Your mate options."

"What if I don't want any of you?" I asked, despite the thoughts already going through my mind about having them as my mates. They were the Four Warlords after all. Any woman would be lucky to have them.

He smirked. "Don't kill our relationship yet, Elara. We only met yesterday."

It didn't feel like it, though. I felt like I had known Venali my whole life.

"Sorry," Durlan said as he appeared beside us. "It took me a bit to find Kydrus."

Kydrus narrowed his eyes and walked up to me. I took a single step back out of nervousness. He stopped. "Why were you crying?"

"Let's go," I ordered them, turning to face Durlan. "I'll explain everything when we get there."

"Any dangers we should be prepared for?" Venali asked.

"Swords at the ready," I said with a nod.

All four widened their eyes and cast glances at each other.

I didn't really think there would be trouble, but I'd been gone a long time. I wasn't positive what we'd be walking into.

I set my hand in Durlan's. "To the castle courtyard, please."

Venali took my other hand, and I avoided eye contact and hoped my cheeks weren't as read as they felt.

We teleported to the courtyard and I snickered at how destroyed it appeared.

"You're laughing at the castle being destroyed?" Amrynn asked.

"Show yourself!" I yelled and moved away from the warlords. "I know you're here! Show yourself!"

Venali stayed close to me, his sword drawn.

"I sense no one," Amrynn said.

I turned to face Venali. "I need you to stay with them. I need space."

"If I'm too far, someone could—"

"Please," I interrupted him.

He scowled, but walked backwards until he was beside the others. They all stood in a large circle with their swords drawn.

I walked closer to where the front doors used to be.

"Elara," Venali growled.

"Stop hiding!" I snapped. "You know I hate it when you hide from me."

A deep male voice chuckled. "You kept me waiting a long time," the voice said.

"I was frozen, if you recall, and when I woke up, I had no memories. You said that wouldn't happen," I yelled back.

"Who is it?" Kydrus asked.

"How did you manage to gather the Four Warlords?" the invisible man asked.

I sighed. "Come on. Drop the glamour."

"But look at their confused faces. This is much more fun."

"Ryul!" I growled.

Large arms wrapped around me, and the illusion fell.

CHAPTER 7
ELARA

The Four Warlords of Minloa were torn between disbelief at the pristine state of the castle, and fury at me being held by a man they didn't know.

To be fair, I had no idea how trustworthy Ryul was now. He could want to kill me for all I knew.

The instant that thought crossed my mind, my entire body tensed.

Ryul's large, muscled arms tightened a moment before he turned me to face him. The last time I had seen him, he'd been a gangly ten-year-old boy. Ryul had grown in the thousand years we had been apart into a well-muscled and handsome man. The glint in his eyes let me know the mischievous boy was still in there, though.

He frowned, his brows furrowed. "What's wrong?"

"Are you mad at me?" I asked softly.

His brows smoothed out, and he rested his calloused hand on my cheek with a smile. "I would wait ten thousand years for you, my queen."

His head lowered towards mine, and my heart beat faster. He was going to kiss me.

Kydrus pulled me back, while Venali slammed into Ryul's side, pushing him away from me.

Ryul spun around Venali with a speed that seemed impossible and punched him in the face. Ryul drew his sword and turned towards me and Kydrus. "Release Queen Elara!"

"Who are you?" Venali demanded, his grip on his sword so tight that his knuckles were white.

Ryul growled and advanced on Kydrus, his body glowing and blue flames slipping down his blade.

I had to stop this before they killed each other.

"Stop!" I ordered them.

Everyone froze.

I stepped out of Kydrus's hold and ignored his growl. I placed myself in the center of the five men. "You five will not fight each other," I told them. "You are my guards and need to learn to get along."

"What?" Amrynn asked.

"Sheathe your weapons and dispel your magic," I commanded them.

Everyone, but Venali complied.

"Venali," I said softly. "Ryul is not going to harm me."

"You don't know that. You haven't seen him since you were five years old. He's been away from you for a thousand years. Men change a lot in just one year. He could be your enemy now," Venali said, his lips pulled up in a snarl, showing off his fangs.

"You're right," I said and turned to my old friend.

"Elara," Ryul said with wide eyes.

"But, Ryul swore an oath. He would die within hours of hurting me," I said.

"What proof do you have of the oath?" Durlan asked.

Ryul raised his right sleeve, revealing the symbols magically etched into his skin that glowed a light blue. They were a reminder of his oath. "I am bound to serve and protect Elara, heir of Minloa. If I harm her or cause harm to befall her, my life is forfeit."

Venali's sword lowered. "How old were you when you made that oath?"

"Nine," Ryul said.

"Why didn't you search for her?" Kydrus asked.

"Our agreement was for her to return here. Apparently, someone broke the spell I placed on her, causing it to falter and block her memories." He met my eyes and bowed. "I'm sorry."

"How long would you have left her frozen?" Durlan asked.

Ryul straightened. "She was supposed to wake when the time was right. I had faith she would wake during my lifetime."

"Give him a break," I said to Durlan. "He was only ten years old when he used the spell. How proficient were all of you at ten?"

I walked to Ryul and set my hand on his right arm, over the symbols. They glowed and warmed under my touch.

"I've kept the castle secure. No one has been inside, except for me and the groundskeeper," Ryul whispered.

"We should go inside," I whispered. "We have a lot to discuss."

He took my hand in his, lacing our fingers together, and beamed, his white teeth sparkling and his canines white and sharp. "I've waited a long time to hear you say that."

I wasn't certain how Ryul felt, but it felt as if no time had passed since we were last together. Yet, I knew things were far different now that we were adults.

Ryul waved his hand and the front doors opened. He walked at my side, leading me into the entryway. "Welcome home, Queen Elara."

Everything was exactly as I remembered. The same chandeliers, paintings, and floors of my childhood.

I leaned my head against his shoulder and exhaled. "It's good to be home."

Ryul led the way to my father's war room and pulled out the king's chair.

I stared at it. The lion's head at the top of the chair looked smaller than I remembered it. I ran my fingers over the carved lion's paws, recalling sitting on my father's lap during his meetings.

I sat on the red, cushioned seat, and looked at the map, which had new markers since the last time I had been here. Ryul had added the new cities and indicated where the four sectors were.

Ryul sat on my right, and the others took seats as well.

"Who killed them?" I asked, looking at Ryul.

"Feno."

"You're sure?" I asked softly, trying to control my rage and pain.

"Yes."

Feno had been my father's guard. He had been like an uncle to me. Why had he betrayed them?

The table and bookshelves began to shake as angry tears slid down my face.

Kydrus pushed my chair back, ignored Ryul's growl, and picked me up into his arms, hugging me tightly. "Elara, we will find him and make him pay."

I sobbed, turned my head into his chest, and let the tears fall. Not at Feno for his betrayal, but for the loss of my parents. They had loved me more than anything. That's why they had snuck me out of the castle with Ryul when they learned of a plot against them.

The room stopped shaking.

Kydrus sat in my chair and cradled me in his lap while I cried. Once my tears were done, I wiped my eyes with my hand and stood. Kydrus stood and returned to his seat without another word.

"What happened after you were woken?" Ryul asked, his hands in fists in his lap.

I sat in my chair and let my head fall back. "Not many good

things," I admitted. "Some men broke the crystal you sealed me in. Then they sold me as a slave."

"What!" Ryul shouted, his fists coated in flames.

"Show him," Durlan said softly. "He needs to know the full extent of your trauma so he can guard you better."

Venali growled softly, but we all ignored him.

"Show me what?" Ryul asked.

I stood again, and removed my shirt, holding it just to cover my breasts, and turned so he could see my back.

"Who did this to you?" Ryul asked in a dangerously calm voice.

"We've captured him, and he is awaiting punishment," Venali said.

"There are more scars," I whispered as I put my shirt back on. "But, they are on my legs and I would have to remove my pants, which the warlords weren't comfortable with me doing."

Ryul arched a brow. "I find that hard to believe."

I rolled my eyes at him and sat down. "I escaped my owner and lived in Linta," I told Ryul. "Then, a man shoved me off a cliff in an attempt to kill me. Durlan pulled me from the water and saved me."

"She floated from Silpo to Menma?" Ryul asked.

Durlan nodded. "She had been knocked unconscious at some point, had two broken ribs, and a broken arm."

My mouth dropped open. "You didn't tell me that."

Durlan smiled. "You were in enough shock. Plus, I was more focused on getting you to stop fearing us."

"How did you know who she was?" Ryul asked.

"I pulled a star from the sky," I whispered while looking at my hands in my lap.

"Oh, boy," Ryul sighed. "I hoped you wouldn't figure out how to do that."

"What else can she do?" Amrynn asked.

"I need to test her, but she should be able to rearrange the stars, space travel, and harness the sun's power."

"The last person who tried to harness the sun's power burned alive," Durlan said with a frown.

That had me looking at Ryul.

Ryul nodded.

"Well, now that I have Ryul, you four won't have to worry about guarding me," I said, looking at them. My chest felt tight as I said it, but I ignored the feeling.

"Ryul being here changes nothing," Kydrus said, the hint of a growl on the edge of his words.

"We are still your warlords," Durlan said.

"You are her advisors, but she has no need for—" Ryul growled, but Venali interrupted him.

"The queen, when unmated, has always had, at a minimum, four guards. You can't truly believe you are strong enough to protect her on your own?" the malice in Venali's voice was unmistakable.

"I could have killed all four of you when you stepped into the courtyard," Ryul snarled.

"Are you so egotistical that you'd risk Elara's life just to keep up your appearance of superiority?" Durlan asked.

Ryul ground his teeth. "Of course not."

"Then it's settled," Amrynn said with a smile. "Our lovely queen now has five guards."

I glanced at Venali, but he wasn't looking at me. So, I turned to Durlan. "What now?"

"I still think you should spend time in each of the sectors," Durlan said. "You have a lot to learn."

"When do you plan to announce her as queen?" Ryul asked, crossing his arms over his chest.

"Once she is literate and is up to date on Minloa's affairs," Durlan answered.

"And, after she's learned to protect herself a bit," Venali added.

"And gotten her powers a bit more under control," Kydrus said.

"I think she should wait until she has chosen her mates before we announce her," Amrynn said.

"Oh, is that all?" I asked with a scoff. "So, when I'm fifty? Or should we wait until I'm one hundred?"

"You've been missing for one thousand years. What's another fifty?" Kydrus asked with a shrug, his face stone serious.

I stood quickly and left the room. "I need some air."

The men began arguing, their voices raising higher the farther I walked. Instead of going outside, I walked to my bedroom. I didn't know how safe the area was, despite Ryul's glamour. It was very unlikely, but Feno could come back.

My room looked exactly as I remembered it. Even my stuffed animals were there. I touched the silver comb Mother used to use each morning on my hair, and felt a deep sorrow, all the way to my bones. She would hum songs while she brushed my tangles, and then braided my hair.

I sat on the thick blanket at the foot of my bed, and closed my eyes.

The warlords were a lot to deal with. Not that I was surprised, but I hadn't expected them to stay once they saw Ryul was here and the type of magic he was capable of.

If Mother were here, what would she say to me?

Probably, "Let the men protect you. They are more experienced and have your best interests at heart."

Dad would tell me to work hard to prove them wrong.

Perhaps, I could do both.

"Elara?" Amrynn called through my door.

I sat up and rubbed my eyes. I had fallen asleep, but I wasn't sure for how long.

"Come in," I called around a yawn.

He opened the door, looked around my room, and then shut the door behind him. "Were you sleeping?"

I nodded. "It's okay. What did you need?"

He sat beside me on the bed and smoothed my sleep-ruffled hair down. "I just came to check on you."

"I'm sorry if I worried you," I said and stretched.

His eyes dropped to the strip of stomach exposed by my raised arms. "We've been treating you like a child, and I am sorry for that. We just want to keep you safe," he whispered and lifted his eyes to mine. "You are important. We tend to lose ourselves to protective instincts and impulses and forget about your feelings. I'll try to work on that."

"Was Venali being honest? About you four being my mates?"

He sighed. "He told you about that?"

I nodded.

"Yes, he was being serious. The four of us are your mates."

"Five," I said.

He frowned. "What?"

"Doesn't Ryul get added to the list, since he is my guard as well?"

Amrynn looked at the door, as if he could see the other man. "I suppose he would make it five."

"That's insane," I told him and stood. Then I began pacing. "Why would I need that many? Mom only had Dad."

"Our species has developed an odd issue. You see, a higher percentage of males are born than females. So, most females not only have their choice of mates, but also of how many mates they want to have. Queens, well queens tend to have a half a dozen or a dozen mates. Kings on the other hand, tend to have one mate. Though, some kings before your father had concubines as well."

I stopped and looked at him. "Really?"

He nodded. "Your grandfather had one mate, his queen, and five or six concubines. He treated them all very well, and from what I was told, loved them all."

"This is all insane," I whispered, resuming my pacing. "How am I supposed to pick between five men?"

"You don't have to pick," Amrynn said.

I turned and stared. I understood what he'd said, about women having the option for multiple mates, but I couldn't see the Four Warlords being able to share a woman. Such powerful men were used to getting their way and had their choice of mates. I knew a dozen women who would throw themselves at the warlords, given the chance.

Amrynn stood with a smile and set his hands on my arms. "You are queen. We are yours. Even if you did decide not to choose one of us as your mate, we'd still be your guards. But, we would all kill for the chance to be your mate."

"Because I'm queen?"

"It may start that way, but we are all incredibly attracted to you. I have no doubt that the longer I am with you, the more I will want you."

"You're warlords. You could get any woman you want," I reminded him, swallowing. He was so close. Just a lift of my toes and I could kiss him.

"We could." He rubbed his thumbs on my arms and whispered, "But, you call to us. Just like we call to you, no matter how much you try to ignore it."

"What is this calling?"

"Power," he whispered. "Those of similar power are drawn together. That's why we don't have mates. You're the first female to rival us in power in a very long time."

He stepped closer to me, his head angled down.

"A queen should never take advantage of her station or power," I whispered, remembering my mother saying that to me on several occasions.

Amrynn smiled. "Do I look like I'm here against my will?"

"What do you want?" I asked.

"For you to give us a chance. To spend time with us and get to know us."

"And?" I asked, knowing there was something else.

He traced my lower lip with his thumb. "A kiss."

I placed my hands on his shoulders, stood on tip toe, and pressed my lips to his.

His lips were even softer than they looked.

When I pulled back, he smiled at me.

"We should find the others," he whispered. "Or, they'll come looking for us."

"One more," I whispered, shocking myself, and kissed him again.

He wrapped his arms around me, and kissed me deeply, supporting my weight easily.

I stepped back and ran a hand through my hair, biting my lower lip to keep from doing or saying something I shouldn't.

He kissed my cheek, opened my door, and bowed. "If you'll follow me, my queen?"

These men were going to be a handful. I wasn't certain I could handle it.

But I was damn well going to have fun trying.

"Lead the way, Warlord," I said, smiling wide.

We walked side by side down the empty hallways. The castle's emptiness bothered me the most.

"You are scowling," Amrynn said, eyeing me.

"It's just so quiet. I miss it being loud and busy."

He reached over and squeezed my hand. "It will be again, soon."

"In fifty years," I scoffed and pulled my hand back to smooth my hair down.

Voices ahead caught my attention. They were in the kitchen.

Amrynn pushed open the door for me, and the four men inside stopped talking to face us.

"What's for dinner?" I asked, hopped up onto the counter next to Durlan, and snagged a slice of cucumber to chew on.

"Stew," Durlan said, smiling at me.

I nodded, grabbed an apple, and then froze. "Where'd the food come from?"

Ryul rolled his eyes. "I've been living here, remember?"

I chuckled in embarrassment. "Right, sorry."

He stuck his lip out in a pout. "I can't believe you forgot about your best friend."

I hopped off the counter, walked to where he was chopping mushrooms, and hugged him from behind. "It wasn't my fault."

He set his knife down, turned in my arms, and lifted my chin with his finger. "I promise I'm not mad. There was a period of time when I was mad, but I had faith you would return to me."

"You have too much faith in me," I told him, staring into his familiar eyes. He had been my best friend. My confidante. The one I could go to about anything. Now, he was a man, a gorgeous man, and a candidate to be my mate.

Wait. Did he even want that?

"Can we talk...privately?" I asked him.

He nodded, took my hand, and led me out of the kitchen and to the dining room. He turned to face me, smiling. "What's up, El?"

"Do..." How was I supposed to ask this?

"Yes," he said.

I laughed. "You don't even know what I'm going to ask."

He shrugged. "It involves you, so the answer is yes."

"What if I was going to ask if you want to clean out my toenails?" I asked with an arched brow.

"Then, I'd take your shoes off and start to work," he said with a smirk. "Though, you used to have really smelly feet, so I'll need a mask."

I shoved his shoulder and laughed. "Punk."

He set his hands on my arms. "Ask."

"Do you have any interest in possibly being one of my mates?" I asked, my body tense with nerves.

He smiled. "Yes."

"You could wait to answer," I said. "Think about it."

"I've been waiting for you over a thousand years. There's no reason for me to hesitate. I would kill a million men for the chance to be considered." His eyes glowed slightly as he spoke, and the conviction in his statement shocked me.

"I'm sorry I kept you waiting," I whispered.

He tugged me closer, stroked a finger down my jaw, and said, "I'm sorry you endured such pain. If I could go back and change things, I would. I would take the pain for you."

I wasn't so sure I would. If I changed the past, would I still have met the warlords?

He lowered his head and kissed me lightly. "We should go back to the others."

One week ago, I was convinced I would be alone forever. Now, I had five men protecting me. Two of which I had kissed today. Life changed so quickly.

"El, are you planning to go to each of their sectors like they want?"

I sighed. "Yes. Part of me just wants to hide here, but I should learn more about Minloa."

"Then, I'm coming with you," he said.

"What?" I looked up at him, not sure I had heard him right.

"It's my job to protect you. I will go with you to their sectors."

"What about the castle?"

"I'll put the illusion up, and the groundskeeper is powerful enough to fend off the occasional trespasser," he said and smiled. "I just got you back. I'm not letting you out of my sight anytime soon. Plus, I want to get to know you. You're different now."

"You're different, too," I said. I wouldn't admit it to anyone, but having him with me would ease a lot of my anxiety.

"Come on," he said with a wide smile.

I followed him back to the kitchen.

The Four Warlords stood in a huddle in the kitchen, and I could smell the food cooking.

"Everything alright?" Durlan asked, his eyes catching mine.

The other three turned to face Ryul and me.

Ryul draped an arm around my shoulders. "Everything is great."

Despite the possessive gesture, I smiled. Everything was alright. At least, as alright as my insane life could be.

"How long until food is ready?" I asked Durlan, shrugged out of Ryul's hold, and jumped up to sit on the counter behind the Warlords.

"Twenty minutes," Amrynn answered.

I kicked my legs back and forth, remembering how I did the same thing as a child while the chef made me a snack.

"Tomorrow, we'll all return to our sectors," Venali informed me. "You'll go back with Durlan."

"Okay," I agreed.

Ryul looked at me, expectantly.

"There's a slight change to plans," I said.

Venali's lip twitched, and he glanced at Ryul.

"Ryul will be accompanying me," I informed them.

They all opened their mouths to argue.

I raised my hand. "This is non-negotiable."

"Why?" Kydrus asked.

"Because I am not going to leave him alone in the castle any longer than I already have. And, having him at my side will ensure I am safe."

"You'll be safe by our sides as well," Venali said with a frown.

I smiled at him. "This is not because I doubt your ability to protect me."

"Very well," Durlan said.

Venali and Kydrys spun to face him.

"But, you will need to follow some ground rules," Durlan added.

Ryul leaned his hip against the counter beside me. "Such as?"

"No killing, unless your life is legitimately in danger," Durlan said and held up one finger.

"Okay."

"You will leave punishment of anyone who attacks Elara to the assigned warlord," Durlan continued and held up a second finger.

"Fine," Ryul agreed, but the tick in his jaw let me know he didn't like that.

"And finally, you will give us five hours each day alone with Elara to train and teach her," Durlan said with a third finger raised.

Ryul's jaw clenched, as did his fists. "Five?"

"Should be ten," Venali grumbled.

"Five hours minimum. We have a lot to teach her, and your presence will be a distraction," Durlan said.

Durlan wasn't wrong about that.

"If I sense her life in danger, I will come to her aid, no matter the time," Ryul said.

"We're capable of—" Kydrus started with a growl.

"Agreed," Durlan said, raising his voice to be heard over Kydrus. "But, if you interrupt more than three times using that excuse, we will lock you up during our sessions."

Ryul's tense shoulders and locked jaw led me to believe he wasn't happy with this arrangement. However, he said, "I agree."

Durlan nodded once to finalize their agreement.

Looking at the other three men, it was obvious they didn't like the agreement either.

Amrynn had turned his back to us, and Kydrus's jaw was clenched so tight that his skin was white.

Venali kept gripping and releasing his sword's pommel like he was debating using it against Ryul.

"Venali," I whispered.

He released his pommel and looked at me. "Yes?"

"Walk with me?" I requested and hopped down. As I headed towards the hallway, I wondered how I would be able to handle these five. They were bound to fight at some point.

Venali walked beside me, his right hand resting on his sword's pommel, but at least he wasn't gripping it anymore.

"I understand this is not an ideal situation for you," I said softly to him once we were far enough away from the kitchen that the others wouldn't hear us. This hallway was one I had used the most as a child. I'd run from my room to the kitchen, or sometimes, I brought my father and his advisors snacks in his war room.

"I don't trust him. You have no idea what he has been up to for the last thousand years. And, I don't like how informal he is with you." Venali's hand tightened on his pommel.

"I've known you for an even shorter amount of time." I stopped and turned to face him, glad he was a bit back, so I didn't have to tilt my head so much. "I have no idea if I can trust you. The four of you, or even one of you, could be planning to murder me."

"I would ne—"

I raised my hand. "I am just pointing out that I am going on a lot of faith with all five of you. The least you could do is try to get along. I don't want you killing each other."

His right hand dropped to his side.

"In one day, my life was flipped upside down. I don't know what to do, so I've put my trust in you all. If I focus on the negative possibilities, I'll go insane. There are too many unknowns. Yes, he is informal with me. But, so are you four. I like it. I prefer it. I want you to be the real you. I want to get to know who you really are, not a courtly shell. How am I supposed to choose a mate if I don't know you? This whole mate or mates thing is really stressful, and it's only been a day! If I have to learn about each sector, learn all the life basics, date each of you, *and* worry about you killing each other, I'm going to die of insanity."

Venali pulled me against him, his arms wrapped around me like a cocoon. "I promise not to kill him unless he is trying to kill you or one of the other warlords. I'm sorry. I didn't mean to add to your stress. And, this is the real me. I'll never be anything else with you."

"Promise?" I mumbled into his shirt. He smelled so good. I wanted to roll in his scent, like a cat in catnip.

He tilted my chin up. "I promise."

I knew it was coming, and yet the kiss still made me gasp. His lips seared mine, and I wondered what it would feel like if his lips touched other places on my body.

Durlan cleared his throat down the hallway.

I stepped back from Venali, my cheeks burning.

"Food is ready," he informed us and went back into the kitchen.

Venali smoothed down my hair and pushed it out of my face. "I'm really looking forward to my month with you."

So was I.

"Come on. I'm hungry," I said with a coy smile.

He smiled back, and we returned to the others.

Our meal was a somber affair, and I returned to my room as soon as I finished eating.

I wanted to be loved. But I was being too forward with them. I barely knew these men. I shouldn't have let them kiss me until after at least a month of courting. Throwing myself at them was not a good idea.

A fun idea, but not good in the long term.

I fell onto my bed with a groan. How was I supposed to resist them when I'd be alone with each of them for a month at a time?

I was a horrible person. I'd remembered I was royalty, and now I had no issues courting five men at once, with the option of keeping them all.

My mother would have fainted if she'd seen me now.

I should enjoy life, but I needed to set boundaries.

Awful, horrible, boring, but necessary boundaries. The queen couldn't be seen making out with men in public. No matter how tempting the men were.

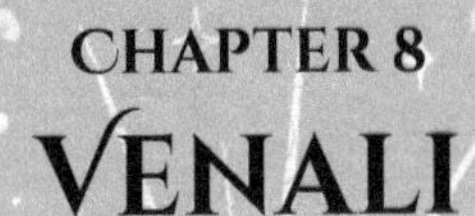

CHAPTER 8
VENALI

SHE WAS TOO TRUSTING, but for some reason I found myself agreeing with her judgment.

Elara was beautiful, smart, and I was falling fast for this young woman. Part of me thought I was thinking with my lower body instead of my brain.

Yet, I also couldn't discount the way she made me feel when I was with her. Or, even when just thinking about her.

No other woman had drawn my attention like her. Sure, I'd slept with other women, but Elara was the type that you wanted to show off and hide at the same time.

I wanted her by my side, to ensure no one ever hurt her again. I wanted others to see me with her. I wanted to hide her from every other man in the world.

She was a fighter and there was a connection between us that I could not deny. That I did not *want* to deny.

I would do everything in my power to keep her safe and happy. Even if that meant sacrificing myself. She would change the world. I could feel it.

I wanted to be by her side when she did, but watching her from the heavens would be good enough for me.

CHAPTER 9

ELARA

"You're going to kill me," I gasped, sitting on the ground outside Durlan's house.

Ryul rolled his eyes. "Stop being dramatic."

Every night, Ryul spent an hour teaching me to control my magic. Apparently, my type of magic was hereditary, and he had done a lot of research on it during the thousand years I had kept him waiting.

"Can't I try planetary travel?" I asked. That would be way more fun than just channeling the stars' power.

"Absolutely not," Durlan said from the chair where he sat, reading a book. He set the book down. "What if you can't come back?"

I tugged on a blade of grass. "Minloa doesn't know I exist yet, so it wouldn't be that big of a deal or loss."

Ryul thumped me on the top of my head.

"Ouch," I hissed.

He scowled down at me. "You are not going to another planet. I'm not going to lose you again."

"I didn't say I was going to," I grumbled.

"Let's stop for the night," Durlan said and stood.

I lay on my back, looking up at the stars. "I'll stay here for a bit."

Durlan sat beside me and began massaging my temples.

I closed my eyes and sighed in pleasure. With so little physical contact most of my life, I craved it now. It was addictive.

"Shooting star," I said, raised my hand, and pointed while keeping my eyes closed.

"What else can you sense?" Ryul asked. "Can you sense the planets and whether there is life on them?"

"There's no life on the three planets closest to us. I can't feel beyond that."

"What type of planets are they?" Durlan asked, still massaging my head, but moving to my scalp.

"Only one of the three are a type we could inhabit. The other two have strange ecosystems. One is really hot."

"Could you draw a map of the system?" Durlan asked.

I nodded.

"Tomorrow, I would like you to do that," he whispered.

"I'm going to Amrynn's in a week, right?" I asked and opened my eyes to look up at Durlan.

"Yes," he answered.

The weeks had flown by. I wasn't sure where the time had gone. I had learned a lot, though. I could read well, and my writing was improving. Durlan had also given me a run-down of the current affairs. Which, to be honest, was boring. My slavery was the most talked about news in decades.

When the time came, Amrynn teleported near us, a smile on his face. "Good evening. Are you two ready to go?"

I hurried inside, grabbing the few items I had brought to Durlan's, and returned to the three men. "Ready."

Durlan pulled me into a hug, and I squeezed him back. "Stay safe and learn as much as you can."

"I will," I said with a salute.

Amrynn held out his hand, and I set mine in it, giving his a squeeze.

Ryul took my free hand, shouldering my bag for me, and saluted Durlan. "See you in a few months."

I smiled at Durlan, just before Amrynn teleported us to his house.

"Welcome to, Blustum," he announced, releasing my hand to gesture down the hallway. "Your rooms await you."

"Same room as at Durlan's?" I questioned, heading down the hallway towards the bedrooms.

"Yes. We thought it might make it easier for you to stay in the same room at each of our houses," Amrynn answered, following me slowly.

Amrynn's house was decorated in blues, reminding me of water and the sky during the day.

"Thank you. I think it will make it a bit easier." I pushed open the door and stared in silence at the room. It had the essentials: bed, dresser, side table. But it also had several clothing racks and over ten pairs of shoes on the far side. "What is this?"

"You don't have very many clothes," Amrynn said. "I thought you might like to pick some out. These should all be your size, but if they need altering, I can summon my tailor. The shoes should be your size as well, but if there is something specific that you want, please don't hesitate to ask."

I was in dire need of some new clothes. Living in Linta, I didn't make much money, and didn't want to spend what I had on frivolous things like clothes. Now that I had access to my wealth again, there was no reason for me not to upgrade my wardrobe.

I turned and hugged Amrynn, pressing a kiss to the side of his neck before I spun back around and started going through the clothes.

"Can I talk to you?" Ryul asked.

I turned, but he was speaking to Amrynn.

"Shout if you need me," Amrynn said, and shut the door with a smile.

I resumed my browsing and then started throwing clothing items I wanted to try on, and the ones I knew I wanted to keep. There had to be over one hundred outfits on the racks. Once I finished making my piles: yes, maybe, and hell-no, I turned to the shoes. I needed boots, sneakers, high heels, and flat sandals.

I looked at the pile of clothes and chose a pretty sundress I'd seen first. I tried it on, slipped on a pair of flat sandals, and stood before the full-length mirror in the bedroom. It made me look feminine and dainty. Old me wouldn't have worn it. But I wasn't that shy, timid girl anymore.

Someone knocked on the door. "Come in," I called while still admiring the dress.

"I was hoping you might pick that one," Amrynn said.

I twirled, letting the skirt flare around me as I turned to face him, a wide smile on my face. "It's beautiful."

He leaned against the doorjamb and smiled. "The woman makes the dress, my queen. And, you far outshine that scrap of cloth."

Amrynn, the wordsmith. He was by far the best with words and knew just how to use them to his advantage.

I'd gotten a bit of intel on him from Durlan before I'd come to prepare myself.

I curtsied and bowed my head. "Thank you."

He took my hand and twirled me around before pulling me

against him in a dancer's hold. "Do you know how to dance, my queen?"

"Elara," I reprimanded him.

He smirked. "Elara. Do you know how to dance, Elara?"

"I remember a little from when I was a girl, but it has been a very long time."

"Then I shall be forced to teach you," he said with a dramatic sigh, spun me, and then dipped me.

When he brought me back up, I smiled wide, like a lovestruck idiot.

"Tonight, you should rest, though. Tomorrow will be a full day of learning." He bowed over my hand and kissed the back of it. "Good night, Elara."

I watched him leave, warmth blossoming on my cheeks long after he had left. I locked the door, and then flopped down onto the bed atop my piles of clothes. These men were so much older than me, so much more experienced. I was in over my head.

And, if I were being honest with myself, I loved every minute of it.

Quickly, I went through the clothes, tried on the ones I needed to, and then used the racks to separate the ones I was keeping and the ones I would be returning.

As I went to sleep, I pondered over the warlords. I felt no ill will from any of them and believed I could trust them, but could I really? Ryul was the only one I knew without a doubt wouldn't hurt me. The others were old, had much longer lives behind them, and were well-versed in deceit. They could play a long game of lies and subterfuge, stringing me along until they got what they wanted. I had to ensure that didn't happen. I had to ensure that they did not betray me like Feno had my parents.

Could I convince them to make an oath, like Ryul had?

It would definitely help me sleep better.

I would talk to them individually. I felt certain that Venali would make one as soon as I asked. Kydrus was the one I was most concerned with. He seemed like he cared for me, but he was always scowling when he looked at me. He was always the quickest to anger. Was it because he felt stupid for not realizing who I was? Or was it because of something else?

Politics made my brain hurt!

And, I had only begun to enter the political arena.

"Why couldn't I have been a farmer?" I muttered to myself.

"This is Tre," Amrynn introduced me to a middle-aged man with golden hair. The man stood in the middle of the dining room, which had been emptied of furniture.

Tre held out his hand. "Nice to make your acquaintance," he said in a rich, honeyed voice.

I shook his hand and curtsied. "Nice to make your acquaintance as well, Tre. I'm Elara."

"Tre will be teaching you to dance," Amrynn explained.

I looked at him and he smirked. "Although I would love to teach you to dance, Tre is a much better teacher. I'll assist you with practicing, but Tre will be the one to teach you the steps and moves."

"Okay." I smiled and gave Tre a nod. "Ready when you are."

Tre waved his hand, and a white sphere floated out of a bag from the ground to his hand. He whispered something to the sphere, tossed it into the air, and then music began to play.

My eyes widened, and I stood, mesmerized by the sphere.

"It's my special brand of magic," Tre explained. "It will play the songs for us, and I can make it pause or go back to the beginning if need be."

"That is amazing," I whispered.

He chuckled and looked over my head at Amrynn. "She's adorable. I like her."

"Don't get attached," Amrynn said, smiling wide enough for his canines to show.

Tre rolled his eyes. "You know I don't shop in that store."

I tilted my head and scowled. "What?"

"I prefer men as sexual partners," Tre said, lifting his brow.

"Oh," I said and chuckled. "Shop at that store. That's a good one."

Tre held out his hand. "Shall we begin? Our dear warlord has informed me that you have some basic knowledge of dancing."

I nodded. "I can waltz. Or, at least when I was six I could."

"Six? The last time you danced was when you were a child?" Tre asked, scowling.

I nodded again.

He glared at Amrynn. "Whatever rock you found her under, blow it up. This beautiful woman should be gracing dance floors across Minloa. Don't worry, darling. I'm going to teach you all of our dances, so you can outshine every other woman in Minloa."

"She already does," Amrynn said.

I didn't need to look at him to know he was smiling.

Tre snickered. "Our warlord is besought with you. I don't think I've ever seen him flirt so openly with a woman before."

"He made one comment," I mumbled. "I hardly call that openly flirting."

"For him, it is," Tre said. The music started from the beginning, and Tre led me into the waltz. I followed him, surprised with how easy he was to dance with. He taught me a few other dances, some of which I remembered as well, and then waved behind me. "You dance with her. I may just be too good of a lead."

I expected Amrynn to come, but instead, Ryul took my hand and pulled me into starting position.

"You know how to dance?" I asked.

He smirked. "I was born and raised to become your guard. I've been trained to dance and continued to practice during your absence."

"Who did you practice with?" I asked, trying to hide my smirk and failing.

"I practiced alone," he said.

"Well, let's see if your solo dancing translates to dancing with me." I turned to Tre. "Ready."

Tre started the music, and Ryul led me into the dance smoothly. We spun around the room, and I became lost in Ryul's eyes. He spun me away, spun me back, and then dipped me as the song ended.

The world faded, only Ryul existed.

He leaned forward and placed a gentle kiss to my lips and then stood us both up.

"I don't think she needs anymore dance lessons," Tre said.

I looked up, shocked to see Amrynn standing inside the room, a scowl on his face.

"It appears not," Amrynn finally said.

Tre bowed to me and then left.

"What next then?" I asked Amrynn, smiling wide and trying to dispel the weird tension in the room.

"I'd like to take you out to the city," Amrynn said.

"We aren't announcing her yet." Ryul stepped between me and the warlord. "You showing up with her at your side will draw unwanted attention to her."

"It will be fine." Amrynn frowned at him and reached a hand out to me, crowding Ryul's space.

"I'm—" Ryul began and took a step to the side.

"This is my time with her. You will stay here. She will be safe with me," Amrynn snarled as he took my hand.

"Fine," Ryul huffed and then stomped from the room.

"Can I change first?" I asked.

"What's wrong with your current outfit?" Amrynn asked, looking over my pants and shirt.

"If I'm going to be in public with you, I'd like to at least look presentable," I said, rolling my eyes at him.

He strode towards me, a hunger in his eyes that excited me. "You are one of the most gorgeous women in Minloa. You could wear a burlap sack, and every man will be jealous of me being beside you." He bent and kissed my cheek. "But, if you'd like to change, I will not stop you."

I leaned into his warmth, tilted my chin up slightly and stood on tiptoe to brush my lips against his. "I'll be quick."

I hurried out of the room before I tried anything more with him. I wanted to touch him. I wanted him to touch me. I wanted to do so much, and yet I needed to hold myself back.

Once in my room, I stared at the clothing racks before me. What should I wear? The town would see me at Amrynn's side. Even if they didn't know that he was my guard and possible future mate, I wanted to look as good as I could.

I grabbed the sundress I'd tried on in front of Amrynn the previous night and slipped on the same sandals. After running a brush through my hair, I hurried out of the room, almost colliding with Amrynn who stood outside my door.

"Ready?" he asked, his eyes raking over me.

"One second," I said, walked to Ryul's room, and knocked on his door.

He opened it, a scowl on his face, but when he saw me, the scowl was replaced by wide eyes and a look I couldn't decipher.

"I just wanted to let you know that we are leaving," I said.

He looked over my head at Amrynn. "Okay. I'll see you when you get back."

"Okay." I gave him a quick hug, and then spun away before he could hug me back.

I walked by Amrynn and out the front door, waiting for him to catch up to me.

"This way," he said, hands clasped behind his back.

At his side, we walked away from his house, and towards the main city, Crol, down at the bottom of the hill. Unlike Linta, Amrynn's house was not in the middle of the city. He said he preferred to look over his city and to be able to see the entire area to know where he might be needed.

"Anything I should know? Is Crol different than Linta?" I asked.

"Not that I know of. People are used to me making random visits, but they do tend to come out in droves to see me and talk to me. Just stay by my side, okay? I doubt anyone will try anything, especially since they have no idea who you are, but I'd rather be safe than sorry."

"So, just avoid the glares of the women and stay by your side. Got it," I said with a nod.

He scoffed, but didn't deny it.

The town was comprised of mostly houses with a few lower level store fronts. There was also a healer's hut and a fruit and vegetable market.

A heavenly smell caught my attention, and I tried to discretely sniff it out, but Amrynn noticed.

He smiled. "That's our baker. I'll buy you a pastry when we get down there."

"I love pastries," I said with a wide smile.

"What else do you love?" he asked, turning away from me to smile and wave at a few people outside.

"Swimming, though I'm not very good at it. Listening to the sound of a waterfall, or the sound of rain. Running water, I guess would be a better general explanation. I love sweets but try to avoid them because I got really sick on chocolate one year. I loved dresses as a girl, but most of my life I couldn't afford dresses. I love hugs and hate—"

I snapped my mouth shut. Why was I rambling so much?

"Hate what?" Amrynn prompted, moving a bit closer to me.

"I hate being alone," I finished.

"Amrynn," a tall brunette woman with the most gorgeous figure I'd ever seen called out.

Amrynn stopped and smiled at her. A full, genuine smile. "Hello, Alicia."

She walked right up to him, gave him a hug, squishing her large breasts against his chest, and then kissed him on his cheek. "Where have you been? You don't usually go so long between visits."

He stepped back from her, his smile still in place. "I've been busy. Sorry if I worried you."

"Oh, who is your friend?" she asked, looking at me down her nose.

"This is Elara. Elara, this is Alicia." Amrynn's smile still didn't falter.

I held out my hand, smiling politely. "Nice to meet you."

"Did you take in another stray?" Alicia asked with a scowl at Amrynn, ignoring my hand.

I dropped it but kept my smile on. "Don't worry, I'm only here for a couple of weeks. Then, I'll be out of your hair."

"Oh? Are you a relative?" she asked, eyebrows raised.

"No," Amrynn and I said at the same time.

"I'm giving her a tour, so you'll have to excuse us. I'll come see you another day," he told her, placed his hand on my lower back, and gently pushed me forward.

We walked away from her, and I could feel her eyes like daggers in my back.

"So, why aren't you mated to her?" I asked. I'd wanted to be nonchalant but decided for blunt instead.

"She's too aggressive, as you found out. She thinks she is better than others, and that's not something I like. I've told her on several occasions that I'm not interested in mating with her, but she hasn't taken the hint."

Instead of responding, I walked up to the nearest vendor and perused their wares. The fact that he would turn down a woman as gorgeous as her, surprised me.

Then again, he hadn't said that he hadn't slept with her.

My guards were all over one thousand years old. I didn't want to know how many sexual partners they had had.

It was certainly far more than my number...two.

"See anything you like?" Amrynn asked over my shoulder.

"Everything is lovely." I smiled at the seller before walking back out to the main street.

"What's troubling you?" he asked softly, drawing closer to me.

"Just frustrated that I'm so inexperienced compared to you five," I whispered.

"We're at your service. Our experience will help us better assist you," he whispered back.

Naughty images filtered through my head of ways his experience could assist me. I coughed and lowered my head so my hair would cover my face and the blush that was there.

"So, what about those pastries?" I asked.

When we returned, Ryul sat on the front porch with his sword in his lap, polishing it. He didn't even look up before asking, "Did you have a nice time?"

"I did." I sat beside him. "But, sandals were not the right choice for so much walking."

Ryul sheathed his sword, snatched my legs, spun me sideways, and removed my sandals all before I could yelp. His warm hands began massaging my feet, and I moaned as I closed my eyes.

"Your feet are still stinky even after a thousand years." He huffed a laugh.

Eyes still closed, I smacked his shoulder playfully, a smile on my lips.

"Can I skip practicing tonight?" I asked Ryul, opening one of my eyes just a slit to be able to see him.

He chuckled. "No. You need to constantly work on your powers."

"Why? It's not like I use them for anything."

"Not yet, but you will. At some point, you will find the power almost too irresistible and will want to use it. I want to get you as prepared as I can, to keep you from destroying our planet or any nearby planets," Ryul said as he continued working on my feet.

"That would be very unfortunate," Amrynn said, leaning against the front of his house. "I rather like our planet."

"Are you ready for dinner?" Ryul asked.

"Yes, please." My stomach growled at his question, luckily it was too soft for him to hear.

"You cooked?" Amrynn asked, an eyebrow arched.

"I lived alone in the castle for a thousand years. I had to learn to cook," Ryul said with a shrug and put my sandals back on.

"I lived alone and only learned how to roast a rabbit," I muttered as I wiggled my toes, stood, entered the house, and headed for the dining room.

"You didn't have a kitchen like the one in the castle," Ryul said, catching up to me.

"True." I sniffed the air, not hiding the gesture this time.

The smell emanating from the kitchen told me that Ryul had learned to cook well, and I was really looking forward to tasting his food.

I sat at the dining table, knowing he wouldn't let me help him, and waited as he set a covered plate before me. He removed the cover, and I stared in disbelief at the roasted potatoes, chicken, and cooked carrots. It was plated just like our chef used to make them when I was a child.

"This looks amazing," I said with awe.

"Hopefully, it tastes at least as good as it looks." Ryul's eyes sparkled as he gave a bow. "Enjoy your meal."

He started to walk away and I called after him. "Wait. You're going to leave me to eat alone?"

Amrynn sat down beside me and smiled. "Of course not. I was just washing my hands."

I looked down at my dust covered hands and grimaced. "I should do that as well."

I hurried to the bathroom, washed my hands, and then returned to my seat and dug in. Amrynn and Ryul sat with me, but neither ate anything.

"Did you two already eat?" I asked between bites. "Amrynn, you were with me. You didn't have dinner yet."

"I'll eat in a bit," he said. "I like watching you enjoy your food."

"I ate earlier." Ryul shrugged. "I had to try the food and make sure it tasted good."

"It's amazing," I said and smiled at him. I resumed eating and felt a little warmth return to my normally cold heart. Having people to eat food with was a minor thing, but it meant the world to me.

"There have been reports of attacks on the ocean a few miles from shore," Ryul told Amrynn.

"How many?" Amrynn asked.

"Five in the past week," Ryul answered. "They're taking the supplies from the ships and then destroying them.

"Do their attacks seem to be making any patterns?" Amrynn asked, his brows furrowed.

"Not that I know of, but I don't know your area well," Ryul said.

"Wait. Why are you telling him about events in his own sector?" I asked.

"We found it was easiest if Ryul helped with requests for help while you are training with us," Amrynn said. "He can handle minor issues or bring up issues like this one to me. We don't want to leave you unguarded, so there will be times when one of us must leave to handle whatever is going on."

That made sense. Ryul was strong enough to be a warlord, and could handle whatever the other warlords could. But, it bothered me that they had to split up duties like this because of me.

"What do you want to do?" Ryul asked Amrynn.

"I'll go down and take a look at what's going on. I suspect pirates. If that's the case, I may need more than just the two of us to take them down. The last pirate crew I ran into had several strong members." Amrynn cringed as he recalled the memory. "I'd rather be over prepared than underprepared."

"Agreed." Ryul glanced at me. "Would you prefer Venali goes with you or stays with Elara?"

"Venali?" I asked.

Amrynn nodded. "He's our best fighter. I generally call him for backup when fighting tough enemies. In this case, I could have him stay to protect you instead, though."

"Oh, okay," I mumbled. I would rather go with them, but I knew that would never happen.

I took my plate to the kitchen and washed it.

When would I be useful? When would I be able to take the throne and work towards protecting Minloa? I wanted to do it now, but there was still so much to learn.

"I'll go talk to Venali," Amrynn said, walking into the kitchen. "Ryul will stay with you."

I turned and smiled. "Okay. See you when you get back."

He leaned down and kissed me. "I'll come back as soon as I can."

I watched him leave with my jaw barely staying closed. They were being so forward with me. Kissing me like it was something we just did now.

Was it? Was kissing just something we did now?

Not that I was complaining, but normally people waited a month, didn't they? I hadn't exactly been part of the courting ladies, so I didn't really know.

"El, what's going on in that head of yours? Your facial expressions are all over the place," Ryul asked as he entered the kitchen.

"There's just a lot for me to learn." I chewed my lip, half answering him.

"Come on, I want to give you something." Ryul gestured for me to follow and walked out of the kitchen.

I hurried to catch up, biting my tongue to keep from asking what it was. I hated surprises.

Ryul walked into his room, leaving the door open behind him. I hadn't been into his room, or any of the warlords' rooms. I hesitated at the door, looking in and watching him riffling through his bag.

He turned, a book in his hand, and smirked. "Afraid?"

I scowled. "No."

He held out the book, standing in the middle of his room.

It was just a room. Yet, it felt like so much more. It felt like this step meant something. It felt like this was a milestone in our relationship.

Ryul kept watching me, his smirk still in place, and hand raised with the book.

I wanted this. I wanted to move forward with Ryul. With all of them.

With a small step, I entered his room. Then a few more steps brought me to him and the book, which I took. There was no title on the outside.

"What is it?" I asked, opening the first page.

"History of Minloa," he answered. "I found it in your father's study."

"You totally snooped through the entire castle, didn't you?" I asked with a grin.

He shrugged. "What else was I supposed to do for a thousand years?"

Good point. I totally would have snooped, too.

"I haven't read much of it, but it dates back thousands of years before your father was crowned," Ryul said, looking between me and the book in my hands.

I closed the book, and took it to the living room so I could get comfortable and read.

"Do you want a snack?" he asked.

"We just ate." I said, a hand on my belly, but my eyes remained on the book. He didn't respond after a minute, so I answered, "Yes."

I heard his chuckle, but it was far away, likely in the kitchen already.

Stacking up pillows, I got comfortable, and started reading.

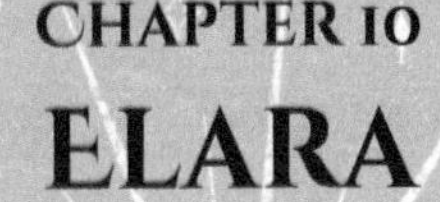

CHAPTER 10
ELARA

"How long has she been reading?" Amrynn asked when he returned with Venali sometime later.

I ignored him, engrossed in the history of Minloa. Of things I had never even dreamed of being possible. Our version of Minloa was drastically different. How had things changed so much?

"Four hours," Ryul answered around a yawn. "I was expecting her to fall asleep, but she hasn't put it down."

"Can't. Too interesting," I muttered, giving them my first response.

"She is alive!" Ryul exclaimed. "I thought she'd turned into a vegetable."

"Do you know what a shapeshifter is?" I asked, setting the book down to look at the men.

"Something that changes its shape?" Venali guessed.

"A person, who can turn into an animal and vice versa. They often exhibit animalistic behaviors as well. There are werewolves, werelions, werepanthers, and so much more!" I exclaimed.

"I've never heard of that before," Amrynn said and glanced at Venali.

"Me neither. What book is that?" Venali approached, a hand out towards my book.

I pulled it close to my chest. "You can't have it."

He smiled, sat down beside me on the couch, and said, "I just want to look. You can hold it out towards me if you don't want me to touch it."

I did just that, turning the book so he could see the passage I was reading.

"I recognize that handwriting from several of my scrolls. I believe this may be a legitimate historical document," Venali mumbled. "Durlan would be able to tell us once he touches it."

"Where did they all go?" I asked softly, resuming my reading.

"We're going to go to my study and discuss strategies for tomorrow," Amrynn said.

I waved. "Have fun."

Venali was the last to leave, lingering a bit. "You look well," he finally said.

I realized I hadn't even said hi to him. After setting the book down, I rose and hugged him. "Hi. I'm sorry. I wasn't trying to be rude. I'm just really interested in the book."

He hugged me tightly and bent to kiss my cheek. "It's alright. I know better than to come between someone and a good book. I still have a scar from the time I interrupted Kydrus." He kissed me again and said, "I'm looking forward to spending time with you tomorrow."

"Same," I breathed, hoping he couldn't hear how hard my heart was pounding.

He left me then, a smile on his face, and I returned to my book. I needed to find out what had happened to the shapeshifters.

"Alright, that's enough for tonight," Ryul growled and picked me up from the couch.

I clutched my book to my chest. "One more chapter," I begged.

"You're drooling on Amrynn's couch. You look undead. It is time for you to sleep. Just think, the sooner you get to sleep, the sooner you can wake up and read."

He had a point.

"Fine," I said and yawned, stretching my arms up over my head, and avoiding smacking him in the head as he carried me.

"You going to be alright without me tomorrow?" he asked.

"I'll have Venali to keep me company." I yawned again. "Just, be sure to come home tomorrow night. Unharmed. Okay?"

He set me down at my door and gave me a grand bow, complete with flourish. "As you wish, my queen."

I grabbed him for a quick hug and then shut my door.

I woke the next morning to Venali cooking in the kitchen. I sat at a stool, watching him.

"They left really early, and didn't want to wake you," he said.

"I figured they would sneak out early," I replied with a shrug. "It's okay."

"How do you like your eggs?" Venali asked.

"Uh, I don't know," I answered. "Cooked?"

He chuckled. "Okay. My choice, then."

He moved about the kitchen expertly, never dropping anything, or looking for something. He just grabbed what he needed and used it. Would I be like that some day?

When he finished cooking, he carried two plates to the dining room, and sat beside me as we ate. I'd expected him to sit across from me, but I actually preferred him sitting next to me.

"These eggs are really good," I said around a mouthful. They were mixed together instead of fried, like Ryul usually made them.

"I'm glad you like them. We call them scrambled eggs," he said. "They're my favorite. Especially, when put on a sandwich."

"Sandwich? That sounds good."

"Maybe I'll make you one for breakfast tomorrow."

"You don't think they'll be back tonight?" I asked, worry gnawing at me.

"They may spend most of today just searching for the pirates," he said, offering a reassuring smile. "Don't worry, Amrynn can handle himself. And, Ryul seems like he can as well."

"I hope so," I muttered. "Maybe it would be better if you went with them? I can just stay here? Or, you could take me to Kydrus."

"Are you trying to get rid of me?" he asked and stuck his lip out in a pout.

I scoffed. "That is not the case, at all." His lip looked so plump. I wanted to touch it, to see if it was as soft as it looked.

He stood, took my empty plate and his, and went to the kitchen.

I grabbed the history book from my room and sat on the couch in the living room, resuming my reading. There had been a war between the shapeshifters, Unseelie, and Seelie fae. I wanted to find out what the ending was.

Venali sat beside me, draping his arm around my shoulders, and began reading a book of his own. I tried to glance over at the book, but he had it angled in a way that I couldn't read it.

I closed my book and examined him. He looked well-rested and completely relaxed. Did he enjoy peace? He was their best fighter, and from the few Seelie fighters I knew, they preferred battle to peace.

My fingers reached towards his scar on impulse, but I froze and jerked my hand away.

He raised his eyes to mine. "You can touch the scars. They don't hurt me anymore."

"What happened?" I asked.

Scarring a fae was very difficult. It had to be a really deep cut that a healer was not nearby to heal, or done with a blood blade. Supposedly, all blood blades were destroyed now.

"During the Great War, I fought an Unseelie general named Lance. He was vicious, fast, and reveled in torturing his victims. He killed one of my friends before I could get there. We fought, and I realized one of the reasons he was able to defeat so many Seelie. Blood blades. He'd had blood blades attached to the tips of his fingernails. So, whenever he scratched you, the wounds bled profusely, and it cost you a lot of your strength and stamina."

Tucking my legs beneath me, I turned to face him, sitting up, engrossed in his story.

"I'd just sunk my blade into his stomach, when he tried to scratch out my eye."

I looked at the magenta eye, glad that such a beautiful eye hadn't been taken.

"I had to stab him again to kill him, but he left me with these mementos to remember him by."

I reached out and traced his scars with my fingertips. Had he scratched Venali earlier in the battle, Venali may not have lived to tell the story.

Venali closed his eyes as I traced the scars, his breath hitching a moment.

"I'm glad you killed him, and that you survived," I whispered, dropping my hand to his chest.

He rested his hand over mine and opened his eyes. "Me, too."

Our lips met, but I wasn't sure who had initiated the kiss. It didn't matter. I was just glad that we were kissing. He wrapped his hand around the back of my neck and deepened our kiss, his tongue sliding along mine.

I moaned into his mouth, and he growled in the back of his throat.

Normally, that would have frightened me, but I knew Venali wouldn't hurt me.

I slid onto his lap, slipped my fingers into his thick hair, and kissed him ferociously. He tasted like smoke and pines. It was intoxicating.

"Elara," he whispered, pulling back from the kiss. "I need to ask you something."

Warning bells rang in my head. I sat back beside him on the couch. "Okay?"

"Are you going to be okay with having multiple mates?"

I blinked. "Am I going to be okay? Shouldn't I be asking you that? Are you going to be okay sharing me?"

He smiled. "As long as I can claim a piece of your soul, I will be happy."

He already had it. Which was absurd, since I barely knew him. Yet, he did.

"I need to ask you something," I whispered, gnawing on my lower lip and avoiding his eyes.

He tilted my chin up with his forefinger. "Ask."

"Will you take an oath for me? The same one Ryul took?"

"Absolutely," he said with a nod.

I'd expected hesitation. A moment for him to debate his answer. But, he'd answered almost before I had finished my question.

"Really?"

He smiled and brushed his lips across mine. "I already plan to keep you safe. The oath will make you feel better, which will help our relationship. I have no plans to ever hurt you, so the oath will not hinder me in any way."

"What if you decide you don't want to be my warlord? Or don't want to be my mate?" I asked.

"If you decide you don't want me as a mate, the oath will still not hurt me. If I go insane and try to hurt you, I want the oath to kill me."

"I don't want you to die," I whispered, the thought bringing tears to my eyes.

He kissed each of my eyes, clearing away the tears. "We all die eventually, Elara. I will make the oath. Would you prefer Kydrus officiates it?"

"Kydrus?"

He nodded. "He is well versed in oaths."

"Okay." I hadn't really spoken to Kydrus much. I was certain he was mad at me.

"What is it?" Venali asked, staring into my eyes.

"Have you talked to Kydrus? Since you guys found me?"

He nodded. "Several times."

"Is he...mad at me?"

He smiled. "No, but I think Kydrus should answer your questions when it comes to how he feels. Come, let's go visit him. We can kill two birds with one stone."

He stood, picked me up as he did, and teleported us to Kydrus's house, right into his living room.

"Kydrus?" I called, climbing out of Venali's arms and walking into the hallway. "Are you home?"

"Elara?" he asked, coming out of his study with a deep scowl. "What's wrong? How did you get here?"

"I brought her," Venali said and stepped out into the hallway. "There's no emergency."

Kydrus's scowl lessened. "Oh. Did you need something?"

I looked down at my hands, which were tugging on the end of my shirt. I'd been able to interact with the others much more easily with my memories back. But, when it came to Kydrus, it just wasn't the same. We had a history. One where I had been a royal pain in his ass.

"Go on," Venali urged. "He's not going to hurt you. Are you, Kydrus?"

"I'll never harm you, Elara," Kydrus whispered. "You know you can ask me anything."

"I'll just wait in the living room," Venali said, abandoning me to the hallway, alone with Kydrus.

"Are you mad at me?" I asked Kydrus. "I know I lied. I know I hid my powers, but I really was scared." I looked up at him, tears shimmering on the edges of my vision. "I really believed you might kill me for my powers."

Kydrus took a slow step forward, and then another, approaching me cautiously since I often flinched or shied away from him. He reached out, took my hands, and squeezed them gently. "I'm not mad at you. I was never mad at you. I was hurt that you thought I might kill you, but when I looked at it from your perspective, I understood. You viewed the warlords as terrifying men with magic rivaled by few. You know our job is to keep the peace, and your magic is one that could cause a lot of issues. I was hurt that you didn't trust me, but I understand. I didn't at the time. Can we talk in my study a moment? I have something I want to tell you."

"Venali, we're going to talk in his study a moment," I called out.

"Okay. I'll just read while I wait," Venali called back.

Kydrus waved me to his study, and I walked into the familiar room, sitting in the chair I always sat in. Today, however, Kydrus chose to sit in the chair beside me instead of his chair behind his desk. "I'm sorry for not protecting you adequately when you lived here," he said. "Had I known how poorly the others were treating you, I would have done more."

"I didn't want you to know," I admitted to him. "I felt like a burden to you already."

He smiled, and it stole my breath. "You were never a burden or a bother. You were one of the few bright moments in my time here as warlord. When I saw you fall off the cliff, I feared you might be gone forever. I tried to find you, but you were swept away too quickly. I'm sorry that I wasn't there to protect you."

"You can't always be by my side," I reminded him. "Plus, I didn't think anyone would actually try to kill me."

"They're jealous of you," he said.

"How?" I asked, an eyebrow arched.

"You're beautiful, you catch the eye of anyone you pass by, and you draw people to you. Many people don't like that. They don't like being drawn to a person. Had they known you were royalty, they would have understood. Your bloodline draws us, makes us feel safe and happy, because you are destined to rule us."

"I think destiny is a dick," I mumbled.

Kydrus laughed, and I startled. I hadn't heard him laugh before.

"I should have recognized who you were, but I chalked my draw to you up to just who you were. You've always drawn me."

"You never said anything," I whispered around a gulp.

His smile wilted. "You were always scared of me. Worried I was going to hurt you. I didn't want to try to kiss you for fear it would be using my title to make you do something you didn't truly want to do."

"You...wanted to kiss me?" I asked.

He brushed his fingertips across my cheek. "Since I first saw you."

"I...I don't know what to say," I admitted.

"May I kiss you?" he whispered breathlessly, his eyebrows furrowing slightly as he focused on me.

I leaned forward and pressed my lips to his. He hesitated a moment, and then returned the kiss, gently and carefully, like he thought I might run away.

Scooting forward on the chair, I found his hands, pulled them around to my back, and kissed him again.

He hugged me against him, pulling me practically into his lap as he kissed me.

"I'm sorry that I hurt your feelings," I whispered when we separated. "I never intended to do so."

"Was this the reason you came to see me? Or was there something else?" Kydrus asked.

"I'd like you to perform an oath binding on Venali," I said. "He's agreed to it."

"Like Ryul's?"

I nodded. Good guess.

"Venali," Kydrus called and stood, going to his desk and taking something out.

Venali entered, looked over my face, focusing a bit on my lips, which were likely red from our kissing, and then smiled.

Smiled.

"You ready to perform the oath?" Venali asked, moving his gaze to Kydrus.

Kydrus set a stick on his desk, and a bowl. "Yes. Where are we putting the markings?"

"I figure the same place as Ryul's works," Venali said. "Someplace visible."

"It will glow when you're near her, which might blow her cover when she comes to your sector," Kydrus said.

Venali shrugged. "They'll assume I'm courting her, which I am, so I'm okay with that."

Courting. So strange to hear that word in regards to me.

"Alright," Kydrus agreed.

Venali stepped around the desk, standing beside Kydrus.

Kydrus touched the tip of the stick into the bowl which now had a weird ink in it. He spoke in the old tongue, most of which I didn't understand, and began to draw the symbols on Venali's arm. The symbols glowed once finished, and Venali's teeth clenched against the pain. Ryul told me that it felt like they were slicing his skin open with fire when he'd had it done.

I stepped forward, placed my hand over the symbols when the last one was drawn, and waited as Kydrus finished with a question.

Venali responded, "I make this oath of my own free will and agree to all terms."

Power zipped through me, making me gasp, and then the symbols glowed so brightly that I had to close my eyes.

The glow stopped, and I removed my hand.

"My turn," Kydrus said.

"What?" I asked, looking up at him.

He smiled. "Venali came to me because he can't perform the spell on himself. But he can perform it on me."

"You don't have to—"

"I know, but I want to," Kydrus said. "Hopefully, it will help you to relax around me a bit more once you know I won't and can't hurt you."

Venali took the stick from Kydrus, and we repeated the procedure.

Once done, I stared at their arms. They'd really done it. They'd really made an oath to never harm me. I couldn't believe it.

I threw my arms around Kydrus first, and then Venali. "Thank you," I whispered to them, tears leaking from the corners of my eyes.

"We would do almost anything you asked of us," Kydrus whispered and wiped one side of my eye.

Venali wiped the other side. "We will always be here for you."

I had no words to reply to them. How does one reply to such devotion?

"Would you like something to eat?" Kydrus asked.

"Actually, we should head back to Amrynn's. I don't know when they'll be back, and I don't want them to freak out if we aren't there," Venali said.

"He's right," I admitted with a sigh. I hugged Kydrus again and brushed my lips gently across his. "Thank you, again."

"I'll see you soon." He offered another smile that made my breath hitch.

I stepped back, took Venali's hand, and waved to Kydrus before Venali teleported us back to Amrynn's.

Venali sat in one of the giant reclining chairs, and without asking, I sat in his lap, angling my body a bit so that we were both comfortable and could read.

Venali gave me a peck on the cheek and opened his book.

I could definitely get used to this.

We cuddled in silence while we read until lunch. Then he made me lunch despite my protests that I wanted to make something. After we ate, we cuddled together more.

Touching. I loved touching and cuddling.

"I expected you to be more active," I said as I ate a snack he'd just brought.

"Active?" he asked, titling his head as he looked at me.

"You're the best fighter in Minloa. I figured you would be outside practicing or training, but you seem perfectly at ease just sitting and reading."

He smirked. "Even fighters need their downtime. It's good for your mind and soul to take breaks from training. Reading is good for you in general."

"We exiled the shapeshifters," I told him. "And banished the Unseelie to their island."

"What?" he asked.

I pointed at my book. "The Unseelie and shapeshifters fought us. They didn't like that the Seelie were always in control. It caused a war, one that the Seelie won, and we banished them from Minloa."

"There's no way that we used to live side by side with the Unseelie." He frowned. "They're evil."

I shrugged. "It says that we did. That the only reason we

banished them is because of the war and that they tried to usurp us."

"Why would our predecessors live with them?" His brow lifted as he peered at my book.

If they were evil, I wondered that too. But, perhaps the Unseelie weren't as evil as we thought. I knew very little about them, though, to make any determinations or judgments.

"I don't like that look on your face," he mumbled.

"Just pondering questions I don't have answers for," I said. "Don't worry, I'm not going on a journey to find them. I'm just thinking about them."

"If you do decide to run off, take me with you, okay?"

I smiled and kissed him. "Okay. You can be my adventure buddy."

He smirked. "I like the sound of that."

"Have you ever traveled out of Minloa? To one of the other continents?" I asked.

He shook his head. "No. I had heard some traveled out and never returned."

"I wonder what else is out there?" I asked. "What else this planet, Anderelle, has?"

"Can you sense other life forms outside of Minloa?" he asked.

I nodded. "Lots of them, but they're far enough away not to worry me."

"Can you tell what they are? Are they fae?"

I shook my head. "I can't sense what they are, just that they are humanoid. There are actually several other land masses like Minloa where these people live."

"Interesting," Venali whispered, his gaze going distant as his mind wandered.

My mind went to those other places. Did they have monarchies there? Did they also have magic? Where they fae? Or something else?

"It's late," Venali finally said.

"Will you wake me if they return?" I asked with a pout.

He nodded. "I will."

I stood, and headed towards my room but paused. "Promise?"

He smiled. "I promise."

I gave him a smile in return and went to bed, but my mind would not quiet. There was so much unknown out in the world. Out in the universe. It was terrifying and exciting at the same time.

CHAPTER 11
ELARA

Ryul and Amrynn did not return that night. Or the next night.

"Can we please go search for them?" I begged Venali for the hundredth time.

"I'm not putting you in danger. They brought me here to keep you safe." He frowned, but his eyes were sympathetic.

"They might need us! At least go look for them, please. Take me to Kydrus or Durlan."

He pulled me into a hug and stroked my hair. "It's going to be alright. Calm down, sweetheart."

I hadn't realized that I was so worked up until he hugged me. I clung to him and whispered, "Please, Venali."

"Alright. Let's go see Durlan," he said with a sigh.

When we teleported into Durlan's office, he immediately rushed over. "What's wrong?"

"She's fine," Venali assured him. "She's just worried about Amrynn and Ryul. They still haven't returned from their mission."

Durlan's brows furrowed. "They might be having a hard time finding the ship."

"Can you please check on them?" I asked, feeling like I was overreacting now that we stood with Durlan.

"I'll grab Kydrus and we'll go check out the situation." Durlan nodded, his hands clenched into fists. "You two head back to Amrynn's, in case we miss each other and they return."

I hugged him. "Thank you."

Venali grabbed me again and teleported us back. "Go sit on the couch and read. I'll make you something to drink to help soothe your nerves."

A drink wouldn't do anything, but I nodded and sat on the couch.

He returned with snacks as well as tea and set them on the table next to me. Then, he draped a blanket over my legs, and sat beside me.

"Tell me a story?" I asked as I closed my book.

"What type of story?"

I shrugged. "One about you, preferably. I'd like to learn more about you."

He silently contemplated a moment, and then started his story. "I went on a mission once, one I thought I could handle on my own. There had been a rash of thefts in a small village near my home. I went to the village, hid beneath a cloak, and stayed with a poor family. They said they never saw who the thieves were because they wore masks and dark clothes, attacking at night when there was very little light. I hid amongst the shadows, waiting for the thieves to show themselves."

I leaned forward, fully invested in this story, waiting to see what happened.

"I didn't see them," he continued. "But I heard screams coming from the house I had been staying at. I ran as fast as I could, but I was too late. They had killed the family, knowing somehow that I had been staying there. The thieves had also gotten away. Disappeared with no trace of their existence, except for the dead people. I staked the village out for two more nights. Finally, they returned. This time I saw them. There were ten of them. They moved with a stealth spell, which made it harder to see them. However, I'd been trained to see through those types of spells. I charged them, roaring my fury, and cut off two of their heads before they fought back. They'd never had someone able to see them before, so they were surprised, despite my war cry. Once they realized I was able to see them, they attacked. Mind you, I was only twenty or so at the time, so I didn't have the training I do now. I killed two more, but the others incapacitated me. They tied me up and took me back to their cave where they'd been hiding out and storing their loot. And, their other victims."

My hand raised to my mouth.

He exhaled. "They'd been taking women back to their cave. It took me half a day to recuperate. The next half of the day, I watched them and learned as much as I could. While they were sleeping, I managed to free myself from the bonds and freed the women. The men woke up after I'd freed the women, and I had to battle them again. I defeated them, but not without being heavily injured."

I couldn't help myself, I reached out and grabbed one of his hands.

He smiled and patted my hand with a smile. "I didn't know how to teleport yet, so I lay by their fire, their dead bodies around me, and waited for my body to heal itself. Two days later, people from the town came. The girls had returned and told them what had happened. When I didn't return, they feared the worst and came to check on me, prepared to bury my body if need be. I learned then that it wasn't always smart to take on things alone. It is better to be over prepared, than under prepared."

"Did you tell me this story to try to remind me not to run off on my own?" I asked, leaning back with a cocked brow.

He chuckled and kissed my cheek. "My story may have served two purposes. Will you tell me a story now?"

"What kind of story?" I asked nervously. I had more bad stories than good ones.

"Whichever one you are comfortable sharing with me," he said.

"Let me think a moment." I pondered over the stories I had.

He readjusted his sitting position so he could look at me easier.

"When I was a child, I'm not sure what age, my parents took me to the beach. It was my first time. I remember staring at the ocean from the beach, and thinking it never ended. I turned to my mother and asked if the water would swallow us up in the future."

Venali chuckled.

"She assured me that the water would not swallow us up. Once I was assured, I didn't want to leave the beach. I loved watching the waves and listening to them crashing on the sand. I actually fell asleep watching the waves, and my father had to carry me back home."

"They loved you, very much," Venali said softly. "I saw them with you once, and the pride and love for you shone brightly."

"I miss them," I whispered. "I can't believe they're dead. I mean, I know they are, but it's just hard knowing I won't see them again."

Venali hugged me tightly. "I'm sorry."

"You didn't kill him," I whispered, melting against him. "You weren't there to be able to stop it either."

What had happened that night? Where had the rest of the guards been?

"Do you want to learn some fighting moves today?" he asked as he stroked my hair.

I hadn't had a man stroke my hair before. It was very relaxing.

"Not today," I whispered.

He chuckled softly but continued stroking my hair.

"If you could do anything right now, what would you do?" he asked.

Dirty thoughts ran through my head, but I quickly pushed those away. "Visit the beach," I said and laughed. "Talking about it made me remember how much fun it was."

"When you come visit me, I'll take you," he promised.

"If you could do anything, what would you do?" I asked back.

His hand stilled on my hair. "I'm not sure," he admitted. "Right now, I'm pretty content to sit here and pet you."

"I'm pretty content to be pet," I whispered, my eyelids starting to droop.

"You're so beautiful," he whispered in my ear. "You smell amazing, too," he said and inhaled from the top of my head.

"What do I smell like?" I asked, my lower body tightening.

"A goddess," he whispered back, kissed my head, then my cheek, and worked his way down to my neck.

I gasped and arched into him.

"You're such a touchy person. How did you survive living alone all those years?" he asked, sliding his hands down my sides, and then around to the small of my back. He pulled me forward, until I sat in his lap.

"I don't know," I said breathlessly. "I think I may be addicted now. I don't think I'll be able to live alone again."

He slid his hands beneath my shirt, his warm, large palms sliding along my bare skin. "I promise, you won't have to." He kissed my collar bone, making me gasp softly, which then made him growl.

"I shouldn't be so forward with you," I whispered, not moving away from him even a hair. "Even as my guard, I shouldn't be like this."

"You can feel it," he whispered. "The pull. Our connection. I don't know what it is for certain, but it is definitely not just attraction."

"Is it because of the oath?" I asked, but I knew it wasn't. I'd felt it since I met them. I'd just been ignoring it.

"You know it's not," he said, pushing me back so he could look into my eyes. "There's something drawing us together. Part of me thinks that's a sign to run, but the rest of me thinks that part is a coward, and that you're perfect."

Heat rose to my cheeks. "I'm far from perfect."

"Perfect for me," he whispered.

"Venali, we hardly know each other," I reminded him.

"I saw your past. I've glimpsed more than what Durlan showed us. It's part of my powers. I can see your desires, and I know that you are a beautiful woman, inside and out. You want to be loved. You want to help people. You want the life you deserve to have. And I want to give it to you."

His lips crashed into mine, and there was nothing gentle about it this time. He lay me down on the couch, positioning himself above me, and slid up my shirt so he could rest his hand on my stomach. I kissed him back, need and want filling me in equal measures. He brushed his thumb along the bottom of my breast and I gasped as I arched up into him.

I hadn't been touched there before by a man.

He slid his hand up slowly, giving me ample time to stop him, but I didn't dare. He cupped my breast, and groaned into my mouth.

He broke the kiss, pushed my shirt up to expose my breasts, and moaned again. "You are gorgeous, Elara."

I tugged at his shirt. "Fair is fair."

He smirked, removed his shirt, and I let my hands wander over his chest and abdominal muscles. He was so ripped. So much more muscular than most of the men I'd seen in Linta with shirts off.

He cupped a breast in each hand, and slowly ran his thumb over my peaked nipples. They were so sensitive and just his touch made me moan in pleasure. He lowered his head, never breaking eye contact with me, and drew my nipple into his mouth. Once fully inside his mouth, he sucked and ran his tongue over it. I let out a cry and then slapped a hand over my mouth.

He smiled. "Don't be afraid to make noises, Elara. I want to hear you moan and scream my name."

"What if the others come back?" I asked.

"Would you prefer we move this to your room?"

This. What was this?

"I don't think I'm ready for-"

"I know," he said. "I'm not suggesting we have sex. Yet." He picked me up, pressing our chests together, and I wrapped my legs around his waist. My nipples ached as they rubbed against his chest. Then he carried me to my room.

He shut my door behind him, and then lay me down on my bed, immediately taking my other nipple into his mouth.

I arched up into him again, gasping. He slid a hand down between my legs and rubbed me through my pants. He drew his mouth away. "Is this too fast?"

I shook my head, trying to resist from rubbing myself against his hand.

He smiled, kissed me deeply, and continued rubbing me. He broke the kiss to flick his tongue over one of my nipples and then the other.

"Yes," I gasped, giving in and grinding myself against his hand.

"I want you to come for me, Elara. I want you to come, knowing that I was the one who did it."

"Yes, Venali," I answered, gasping in breaths.

His growl was one of satisfaction, and I realized that he enjoyed me saying his name.

I grabbed his hand, slid it into my pants, and moaned as soon as he touched my warm core.

"You're so wet," he growled, sliding one finger in slowly.

"Venali!" I gasped.

He growled, bit my neck, and began pumping his finger in and out of me, while rubbing my sensitive nub with his thumb.

My senses were on overload. I made sounds I had never made before, and then bit his shoulder to stop them.

He licked my neck, used his free hand to squeeze my breasts, and then whispered in my ear, "Elara."

I released his shoulder and screamed his name as stars danced before my eyes and the pleasure crashed over me. I thought it would be a single experience, but it came in waves, and the pleasure began building again as he continued to pump his finger in an out of me.

I thought there couldn't be anything better, and then he slid a second finger in with the first, and I gripped his back with my fingers, trying not to scratch him, but hardly paying attention.

"Say it again," he whispered as he pumped his fingers faster and faster.

The pleasure grew again, and another round of waves crashed over me. "Venali!"

This time, he removed his fingers, and gathered me up, cradling me against his chest, our bare skin touching, and he lay down with me draped across his chest.

We lay together in silence for a long time, my heart slowing and my body boneless in satisfaction.

"What do you think our connection is?" I asked Venali. "And, why didn't it show up all these years that I've been with Kydrus?"

He shrugged. "I don't know. Maybe the time just wasn't right. Maybe you weren't ready."

Ready? How could I have ever been ready for this?

I walked to the living room, put my shirt back on, and then stood with my mouth opening and closing but no sound coming out.

"Hi," Ryul said, while Amrynn smiled at me. Durlan snickered but kept healing Amrynn. Kydrus was nowhere to be seen.

"Uh, how long have you been here?" I asked, heat rising to my cheeks.

"We just got back," Amrynn answered. "Durlan was healing us, and Kydrus went to try to find you."

"Found them," Kydrus said behind me.

I yelped and spun around.

Everyone laughed.

Venali snagged his shirt from the couch and put it on. "So, what happened? Did you catch the pirates?"

Kydrus nudged my hip, pushing me towards the couch. I sat, and he sat beside me.

"It took us two days to find them. When we did, they were ready for us," Amrynn said. He snarled, his lips pulling back to reveal his sharp canines. "We defeated them, but it took a lot out of me."

"I couldn't use my illusion power, since it is still up over the castle," Ryul explained.

"We should hire guards for the castle," I said. "Then, you can take the illusion off."

"What do we tell people who see the castle?" Amrynn asked.

"That we've been rebuilding it because you've found the queen," I said.

"You want us to announce you? Why?" Durlan asked.

"Not me specifically, just that you've found the lost princess, queen, whatever," I said. "I don't think we should hide it. I think people should know that we are going to go back to a monarchy."

"That the warlords are off the market?" Venali asked with a smirk.

"I don't care about that," I said and meant it. I trusted that they wouldn't cheat on me. Not that they were my mates yet, anyway, but yeah. "It's going to take the people a bit to get used to the idea of a monarch coming back. There are going to be some who don't like it."

"Which is why we want to wait until you're ready," Kydrus said.

"Will I ever be ready?" I asked, looking at each of them. "Really? I don't think anyone is ever truly ready to be queen or king. They just take the position and listen to their advisers. And, I have five of the best advisers in all of Minloa."

They didn't look convinced.

"Let me finish my visit here, and then go with Venali, and once I've visited all of the sectors, we can make our final decision," I acquiesced.

"Skipping me?" Kydrus asked.

I looked at him out of the corner of my eye. "I know enough about Silpo for a lifetime."

He hooked his arm around my waist and pulled me close. "I apologized about that."

I kissed his cheek. "I know."

"What happened while we were gone?" Amrynn asked us.

Kydrus and Venali held out their arms, showing the other three the oath marks.

All three of the other men's eyes widened.

"It's not mandatory," I said quickly and dropped my eyes to the floor.

"Would you prefer us to make an oath as well?" Amrynn asked.

I didn't know how to respond to that. I would prefer it, yes, but I didn't want them to think they had to. I wanted it to be their decision. Yes, I had asked Venali, but that was different. Right?

"That's a yes," Amrynn whispered.

Ryul chuckled. "It's okay to tell them how you feel."

"I don't want anyone doing anything they don't want to do," I said, jerking my head up to meet their eyes. "I don't want to overstep my place. I don't want you to do things because I'm technically queen."

"You aren't 'technically queen'. You are queen," Kydrus said, squeezing me. "Even if we haven't told anyone else yet."

"Kydrus, will you perform the oath for us?" Amrynn asked.

"Durlan didn't say he wants to do it," I said quickly.

Durlan smiled and stopped healing Amrynn to face me. "I most certainly will take the oath."

"You don't—"

"We know it isn't required," Durlan said. "We already plan to keep you safe. The oath will help with your peace of mind, though."

Hadn't that been what Kydrus had said? Had they already discussed this without me knowing? Were they already prepared to do this?

"I'm very suspicious of you all," I mumbled, eyeing the five men.

The smiles they gave me were equaling disconcerting.

"Kydrus?" Amrynn asked again.

Kydrus kissed my cheek and stood. "I assume you have everything in your office?" he asked Amrynn.

Amrynn nodded. "I may not be able to perform it, but I have all the supplies."

"Good," Kydrus said and the three of them left.

I walked to Ryul and hugged him. "You were gone too long."

He hugged me back, pulling me into his lap. "I'm sorry. There was no way to avoid it."

"You came back, so I guess I'll forgive you. This time."

"How gracious, my queen." He chuckled.

"I am a gracious queen," I agreed.

"You and Kydrus seem to be better," he said.

I nodded. "We talked and got some things out in the open. Now we are good."

"Good," he said, pushing me back to look at me. "You look happier."

"I feel better. Happier." I glanced at Venali, but quickly looked away. "I'm finally accepting my destiny, I think."

"Elara," Kydrus called. "We need you."

"Oh, right!" I shouted and leapt up from Ryul's lap. "I forgot." I hurried to the office and rushed over to the three warlords.

I set my hand on Amrynn, who was the one making the oath currently, and then repeated for Durlan. Once done, we all made our way to the kitchen for drinks and snacks.

I stared at the five men before me, disbelief, warmth, and so many other emotions swirling within me. I wanted to thank them. I wanted to kiss them. I wanted to do so much, but I just stayed silent and watched them work side by side in the kitchen.

How had I become so lucky?

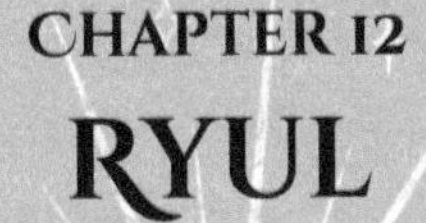

CHAPTER 12
RYUL

I'D WAITED over one thousand years for Elara. All those years, I'd worried that she had died, and that my magic had failed her.

When she'd walked into the courtyard and yelled out for me, I had been certain I was dreaming. Her mother's beauty paired with her father's confidence had turned Elara into a gorgeous woman.

I'd daydreamed about what she would look like, had pictured her when taking care of my needs. But my imagination could not compare to the real thing.

She was beauty personified.

During my time alone, training and intelligence recognizance had been my pastime. To be her guard, her mate, I had to be as perfect as possible. I had to ensure that I did not fail her, as her parents had been failed.

Had I known she would encounter and round up the four warlords, I might have gone to her first. They weren't bad men, but I had envisioned Elara and I being together, alone. Now, I had four other men to compete with for her time.

My protective instincts were gone when around the warlords

now that they had all taken their oaths. It helped me sleep easier knowing that they would not harm her.

I could see she already cared for them and them for her. I knew she cared for me, which was all I needed.

She didn't understand the connection she and I shared. Part of her was still buried, forgotten, and I was worried how she would react when it finally freed itself.

Her magic was powerful, more powerful than it should have been with her bloodline. Her mother had chosen her father to help dilute the magic, but Elara was even more powerful than her mother had been.

I would need to train her extensively, quickly, and ensure she did not destroy us.

Had she known when she was a child about her powers, she could have easily destroyed the men who had kept her as a slave.

My teeth ground together, and a snarl ripped from my throat at the thought of them. Enslaving someone was horrid, but enslaving a child was inexcusable. The warlords had jurisdiction over his punishment, which irked me. I wanted to destroy him, hurt him ten times for every time he had hurt her.

The fact he had scarred her, a Seelie fae, meant he had used a whip laced with magic, or he had whipped her so many times, that it permanently scarred her.

I wanted to kiss every inch of her, to praise her as a goddess, and to show her that her scars mattered not to me. I would worship her for the rest of my days. I would do anything for her.

Even putting up with the warlords.

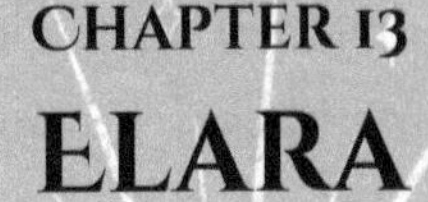

CHAPTER 13
ELARA

"There are two people in an argument, and both are claiming the property belongs to them. What do you do?" Amrynn asked.

Amrynn had begun teaching me about solving disputes. It was boring, frustrating, but totally necessary.

"What is the property?" I asked.

Ryul was in his room, giving Amrynn and I our alone time. Ever since the warlords had taken their oaths, Ryul had been much more trusting of them and willing to give us free time. It was nice.

"A dog."

"Can we make them stand far apart and call to the dog? Whoever the dog goes to wins?" I asked.

He chuckled. "What about if the property was a necklace?"

"Threaten to smash it?"

"Is that a question or statement?" he asked with a chuckle.

"Statement," I said with a nod, though I really wasn't sure.

"What if they both say they don't care or if they both yell out?"

"If they both say they don't care, then I smash it and move on.

If they both yell out, I flip a coin," I said, exasperated. "Do queens really have to deal with this crap?"

"Yes. A lot."

"Maybe I'll make that a warlord duty," I muttered.

"Good luck," he scoffed.

"Shouldn't I learn more about our laws?" I asked.

"Oh, there's an entire book for you to read," he said and laughed maniacally.

"That's such a reassuring and inspiring laugh," I said and stood.

He stood as well, pushed some of my hair behind my ear, and rested his hand on my cheek. "Let's go for a run," he whispered.

"Run?" I asked.

He nodded. "Get changed. Then, meet me back here."

I didn't really want to run, but I changed into my training clothes and sneakers, suspecting there was more to it than what he had said.

I stood in front of my mirror, trying to tie my hair back, but kept missing pieces.

"Want help?" Ryul asked.

I dropped my arms and sighed. "Yes, please."

He took my tie, gathered my hair up, and quickly tied it up. "There you go."

I turned and kissed his cheek. "Thank you."

He pulled me into a hug. "Where are you going?"

"For a run with Amrynn," I answered, breathless from being wrapped up in his arms. He was so handsome. So safe. So...Ryul.

"Train hard," he said, kissed me, and pushed me out of the room with a slap on my butt.

I snarled. "You're going to pay for that."

He chuckled. "Sweet words, with no bite."

"Oh, there will be a bite for you." I growled.

"Temptress." He purred.

I stumbled as I walked away, surprised by his flirting.

"You're keeping him waiting," he called after me.

I growled but hurried outside because he was right.

Amrynn looked me over, heat in his eyes a moment, but when he met my gaze, he extinguished it. "Ready?"

"I guess," I mumbled.

He smiled. "Come on. We will start off slow."

We started off at a slow jog, and he led me into the forests near his place. The animals skittered out of our way but didn't hide. There were several animals I had never seen before. I wanted to stop and ask about them but continued following Amrynn.

There were so many vibrant colors from not only plants, but animals, too.

"It's beautiful here," I whispered.

He sped up a bit. "It gets better."

I picked up my speed, eager to see what else he was going to show me. We ran down the animal trail, dodging low tree limbs, and jumping over fallen logs.

Noise assaulted my ears suddenly, making me skid to a stop. "What? What is that?"

"Come on, you'll see," he said, running again. I ran after him but yelled out when he jumped off a cliff right in front of us.

I looked over and glared down at where he swam in a deep pool of water. It was crystal clear, and we could see all the way to the bottom. The loud noise had been a waterfall that fell into the pool of water.

"Jump in." He waved up at me.

I obeyed, yelling out as I fell, and then closed my eyes and mouth before I hit the pool. The cool water surrounded me, and dragged me down a bit, weighing down my clothes.

I kicked and surfaced, gasping in a breath of air and wiping the water from my eyes.

Amrynn wrapped his arm around my waist, and pulled me against him. "See? This was much better than just running, right?"

"Yes," I said and moved away from him, floated on my back, and closed my eyes. "I missed the water." Lazily, I moved my arms, propelling myself around the lake or pond, or whatever it was.

"This is my favorite place to go. Especially if I need to think about something," Amrynn told me, his voice near my head.

I looked over and found him floating beside me. "Did you need to think about something today?"

"No. I heard that you liked water, and wanted to bring you here. You haven't really had much opportunity for relaxing. Figured it was time for you to have a little bit of fun."

"I have fun with you guys," I said and meant it. They often made me laugh, even during boring lessons.

"What do you want for your birthday?" he asked.

"What?" I scowled. "It's not my birthday."

"Your birthday is in two weeks," he said, frowning.

I dropped my lower legs into the water and faced him. "It is?"

His frown deepened, and he reached for my forehead. "Did your memories not fully return?"

"They are all here. I just didn't realize how much time had passed," I explained. "I thought it was still a month away."

He still looked worried.

"There isn't anything I want," I told him. "I have my memories back and I have you guys."

"There has to be something you want," he prodded.

"I'll think about it," I promised and started floating again.

"If you're unhappy, you can tell us. If there are things you want changed, you can tell us. We want you to be happy. We want to do whatever it is that will make you smile and laugh."

I wrapped my arms around his shoulders and kissed him. "You guys make me happy. I really don't have anything else I want."

"How much greedier could one girl be?" an unfamiliar female

voice asked. "She's stolen our most eligible bachelor, and she still wants more things?"

"Why are you here?" Amrynn asked the girl over my shoulder. I didn't want to turn around and look at her, but my body betrayed me.

"Is this not open land? I'm allowed to walk around here. Or have you passed a new law?" she asked, an eyebrow arched.

She was gorgeous, had large breasts that almost spilled out of the top of her red dress, and long legs that were mostly visible with a huge slit down each of the sides. Her hair was almost silver in color, hung to her waist, and looked silky. Her eyes were full of fire, and I wondered if I could defeat her in a fight. What type of magic did she have?

"You know nothing of our relationship," Amrynn told her. "Do not speak to people as if you know them or what they think or feel."

She walked down to the shore before us. "You visit us less. You were gone, disappeared, for several days without letting anyone else know," she snapped. "You didn't do that type of thing before she came."

Amrynn climbed out, glaring at her. I stayed in the water, not wanting to give up my time yet.

Amrynn's lips were pulled back in a snarl. "I was on a mission for several days. That mission did not involve her. I did not notify any of you, because I had Venali here, watching over our sector. I do not answer to you. I do not have to explain my actions to you," he growled.

She scoffed. "We need to be protected. If you are not able to protect us anymore, perhaps we need a new—"

Her words were cut off by Amrynn's hand around her throat.

"I am Warlord. Not you. If you think you can usurp me, please, try me. If not, then fuck off and leave Elara alone." His teeth snapped next to her face, and she whimpered, eyes wide with fear. He released her, and she ran from the area.

"That was a bit harsh," I whispered.

He sighed. "She needed a strong reminder not to mess with me."

"Well, I think she got the message," I whispered. I got the message and his wrath wasn't directed at me. I was slightly scared. Warlords were frightening men, filled with power. So much power. It was also really sexy. I was a horrible person to be turned on by his anger, yet here we were.

"I'm sorry," he whispered and swam back out to me.

"For what?" I asked, looking down at the small fish swimming below us.

"Scaring you," he said softly. "I don't ever want you to be frightened of me."

I traced the oath symbols on his arm and said, "I know you won't hurt me."

"I wouldn't have even without the oath," he whispered and captured my lips with his.

I wrapped my legs around his waist and kissed him back. His skin was so much warmer than usual. Was it from the sun? Or because the water was cooler.

He drew back. "If I am moving too fast, just tell me. Okay?"

I nodded and bit my lip.

"We should head back," he whispered, but kissed me again.

"We should."

He groaned and pushed me away gently. "If I keep touching you, I won't leave."

I laughed and followed him out of the water and back to his house. I wanted to hold his hand. The thought of that woman, or someone else, catching us had me fisting my hands at my sides instead.

"You're learning really fast," Amrynn said with a smile.

"Thanks."

I didn't feel like I was learning fast. I felt like I had a hundred years of things to learn. Was I going to have the same lifespan, since I'd been frozen? Or, was I already one thousand years down?

"Soon enough, you'll be taking the throne, and you won't have time for us," he said.

I stopped and turned to face him. "What are you talking about? I'll be spending most of my time with you five."

He chuckled. "I'm sorry. You just looked so concerned. I wanted to see if you were listening."

"Of course, I was listening to you. And, I was just thinking about my lifespan," I said and resumed walking.

He fell into step beside me. "Your lifespan?"

I nodded. "Just wondering if being frozen altered it."

"I'll have to talk to Ryul and find out."

We walked in silence, both of us lost in our own minds.

Ryul waved as we approached. "Have a nice run?"

I nodded, kissed his cheek as I passed, and went to the bathroom for a nice, long shower.

Using up all the hot water wasn't my intention, but I dried off quickly, and dressed in new clothes as fast as I could. My fingers were pruned from being in the water so long, but it was so worth it.

"In the living room," Amrynn called to me.

Ryul and Amrynn sat on different couches, Ryul writing a letter or something, and Amrynn with a book.

"What are you two up to?" I asked, running my fingers through my still damp hair.

"Relaxing," Amrynn answered without looking up.

Who should I sit next to? I'd just been with Amrynn, so it should be fine to sit with Ryul, right?

I was about to find out.

Instead of sitting right next to him, like I wanted to, I sat at the other end of the couch, folding my feet up beneath me.

I grabbed my book from where I'd left it on the table and began reading.

Hours passed in silence, and I found that I enjoyed just being near them while I read.

Amrynn cornered me in my room the morning I was supposed to leave to head to Venali's. He slid his hands along my sides, up and down my arms, and then intertwined our fingers.

"Don't be afraid to tell Venali if he is working you too hard. Sometimes he forgets that others don't have the same stamina as he does." Amrynn's words were soft, but his eyes were full of fire.

"Just say it already," I said with a smirk.

His lip twitched as he tried to hold back his smile, but then he gave in and smiled. "I'm going to miss you."

I kissed him deeply. "I'm going to miss you, too."

"You know, you can write to us while you're in the other sectors," he whispered, sliding his hands along my waist.

"I can't write well," I whispered back, my cheeks heating in embarrassment.

"Practice makes perfect," he said, smiling wide.

"Okay," I said with a sigh. "I'll write while I'm with Venali."

"Time to go," Ryul called through the door.

Amrynn kissed me deeply, our tongues intertwining just like our arms.

When he pulled back, we were both breathless.

He stroked my cheek with his fingertips and then opened my door and shoved me out of it. "I'll see you soon, my queen."

Not soon enough.

"Bye," I called over my shoulder and hurried outside to where Ryul and Venali waited.

"Ready?" Venali asked.

I nodded. "Ready."

He held out his hand, and I set mine in it. He gave me a gentle smile, then Ryul intertwined his fingers with my free hand, and we teleported to Venali's house.

"I'll take your bag to your room," Ryul said, releasing my hand and heading towards the bedroom.

"Anything eventful happened while we were apart?" Venali asked, leading me to his study.

I shook my head. "Nope. All quiet on the home front. What about here?"

"Nothing out of the ordinary," he replied, which wasn't really an answer. He sat in his chair behind his desk, and I sat in one of the chairs in front of it.

Ryul entered and took the vacant chair beside me. "Update?" he asked.

"Not much. It's been rather quiet," Venali answered.

"Too quiet?" Ryul asked.

Venali smirked. "I always think it's too quiet, but no. I don't think there is anything brewing. But I could be wrong."

"Let's hope you're not wrong," I whispered.

"Had enough excitement this month?" he asked.

I nodded and yawned.

"She hasn't been sleeping well," Ryul told Venali while looking at me.

"Nightmares?" Venali asked.

"No," I said.

"Yes," Ryul said.

I looked at him. "What?"

"You've been waking Amrynn and I up at night with your cries. You're having nightmares. Amrynn started sleeping in your bed at night to ease your fears, and that seemed to work," Ryul explained.

"I don't remember having nightmares and I sure as hell don't remember Amrynn being in my bed," I said. Not that I would be upset to find him in my bed.

"He left before you woke up each morning. We worried you might order us not to help you, but it was negatively affecting your health," Ryul told me. He turned to Venali. "I recommend you share a bed until we figure out what is causing the nightmares."

"You're okay with me sharing his bed?" I asked, an eyebrow raised.

He smirked. "They're your guards. They're going to be sharing your bed sooner or later."

I was speechless. He'd started off so jealous, but now he didn't mind me sharing a bed with one of them. Such a drastic change.

"Are you opposed to me sharing your bed?" Venali asked. "I can wait until you're asleep, if it would make you feel better."

I looked down, my blush so hot I thought my skin might melt off. "I'm fine sharing a bed."

"Good," Ryul said.

"Would you like to run a perimeter sweep?" Venali asked Ryul.

Ryul yawned. "Not tonight. I prefer to do a sweep while there's light the first time."

Venali nodded. "Smart."

"Can you show me your map?" I asked, still unable to look up at either man, settling for looking at them from my periphery.

"It's behind you on the wall," Venali answered.

I stood, even more embarrassed because I should have actually looked at his office when we entered, but I'd been more enthralled by the owner than the room.

There were a few knickknacks on his desk, but I wasn't sure what any of them were. His walls were lined with swords instead of bookshelves, which seemed rather fitting. One sword had a greenish tint to it, and I moved towards it.

Venali grabbed my wrist, stopping me from reaching the blade. "That's coated in magical poison. If the blade cuts you, you'll die within a day."

I flinched. "Noted. Don't touch green blades."

Ryul snorted behind me, but I ignored him.

Venali kissed my knuckles. "That's a good idea."

I turned to the map, trying to memorize as much of it as I could. It surprised me how alike the sectors were all set up. Not identical, but it seemed like they tried to make them somewhat similar. Was it to make it easier on the people?

"We made the sectors similar so we wouldn't have to worry about having to memorize several maps. It makes visiting each other and looking for each other much easier," Venali said.

I turned and gaped at him. "Did you just hear my thoughts?"

He chuckled. "No. I just assumed that's what you were thinking by the look on your face."

I looked at him from the corner of my eye. I wasn't sure I should believe him or not.

Ryul has a small penis. I thought.

Neither man said anything.

I exhaled a breath and resumed looking at the map. My eye drifted to the map of Minloa, specifically to the barren land around Klinsot and the castle. Was there a way to heal the land? To make it fertile and have acres and acres of crops, like we had when I was a kid.

Something tickled my nose. "Do you have the fireplace on?"

Venali scowled. "What? No, I don't—" His eyes widened, he grabbed a sword as long as he was tall from the wall, and ran from the room.

I ran after him, Ryul at my side. For once, he didn't stop me from running outside when there might be danger.

We stepped outside, and Ryul and I both gasped.

Fire. The town was on fire.

A loud roar had Ryul pushing me back onto the porch, and both of us looked for the source.

Where was Venali? I couldn't see him.

Venali roared nearby, our heads turned, and I gaped in shock.

Venali stood on the ground, holding the giant sword, and facing a real, live dragon.

I hadn't seen a dragon before. The last I'd heard, the warlords had culled their numbers on Minloa, and the only ones left were on different continents.

The dragon was red, easily three times that of an average horse, had spikes all down the middle of its body, and had massive wings, which it had currently flared out to make itself look larger. Not that it needed to look larger.

I wanted to call out to Venali, fear clawing at my chest to see him standing before the huge beast, but if I did, it could distract him. I didn't want to be the reason he got hurt.

"I need to help the town. Stay here, please. Let Venali handle the dragon, okay? Just stay on the porch."

I met Ryul's eyes. "Okay. Hurry." I could hear people yelling for help. "Make sure there's a healer. If there isn't one, contact Durlan."

Ryul kissed my cheek and ran from the house, headed towards the town, which was billowing smoke into the sky from the various fires.

Venali charged the dragon with a focused expression on his face, the dragon opened its mouth, and I bit my knuckles to keep from yelling out. The dragon spewed flames, but Venali slid beneath the fire, and struck with his sword, cutting the dragon's leg.

The dragon roared in pain, swiped at Venali with his other leg, long talons aimed to slice him apart.

Venali rolled away. Then he stabbed the sword into the dragon's side, burying it almost to the hilt.

I could barely breathe. I was so focused on Venali, on this fight, that I didn't care about anything else.

The dragon swung its head to the side and clamped its mouth around Venali, who cried out in pain.

"Venali!" I screamed, running towards him.

Without thought, I drew the power from the stars and our sun and blasted the dragon's eye with the light.

The dragon roared, opening its mouth and dropping Venali. It pawed its injured eye, but I was certain I had permanently blinded him.

Venali hopped up, jerked the sword from the dragon's side, and used it to slice the dragon's head off.

I collapsed to my knees, breathing heavily from using so much magic that quickly, and from relief that he was alive and moving.

Venali walked over, blood dripping from the bite wounds the dragon had inflicted and glared down at me. "What were you thinking?"

I opened my mouth and closed it several times before I could finally speak. "What?"

"You should not have left the porch. Ryul told you to stay there. What were you thinking?" He was snarling at me, his sharp canines shining in the light.

I stood, stared right into his stupid eyes, and said, "I was thinking that you were in a dragon's mouth and I needed to help you, you ungrateful jerk!" I spun to turn away, but he grabbed my arm, spun me back around, and kissed me.

I shoved his chest, and he released me.

"No," I growled.

"I'm sorry," he called after me as I stormed away. "You put yourself in danger. The dragon could have hurt you."

"You were in danger," I said, but didn't turn around to look at him. "I couldn't just let the damn dragon eat you."

"I'm sorry," he called again.

"Go help your people," I ordered him, stomped into the house, and slammed the door behind me.

"Men!" I yelled and then screamed wordlessly.

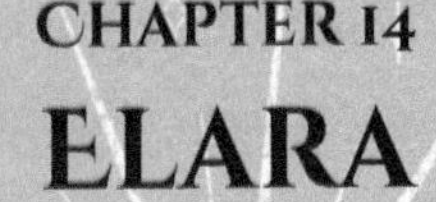

CHAPTER 14
ELARA

Luckily, the dragon caused no fatalities and very few injuries. One house was destroyed, but the owners were assured the house would be repaired within the month.

Venali offered to make a desk for me from the dragon's skull, but I refused. I had no idea what he ended up doing with the skull, or the rest of the dragon, but it wasn't on his lawn anymore.

I was still upset that he'd yelled at me for helping him. Especially, when Ryul had gotten upset with me as well, lecturing me when he returned to the house.

I ignored them for almost a full day, but I was slowly losing my anger, trying to see it from their point of view.

A few days later, and I'd put the event behind us. We had all been amped up in the heat of battle and the thought of losing each other.

"We're going to work on your hand to hand combat today," Venali said after I finished breakfast.

"Okay. I'll get changed." I had decided not to change out of pajamas that morning, because I had been so hungry.

"Meet us in the training ring," he said, eyes intense.

I saluted him as I walked away.

"You need to work on your writing after you train with Venali," Ryul called after me.

"Yes, sir," I called back.

I had sent two letters to Amrynn, but my writing still sucked. I feared I just had poor handwriting. I knew some people who claimed they couldn't improve theirs. What if I was the same?

After changing, I went outside, around the side of the house, down the hill, and to the dirt training arena Venali had. Venali stood in the center, talking to Ryul, who sat on the fence that surrounded the arena.

"We're having an audience today?" I asked, hopping over the fence to join Venali.

"He's going to assist," Venali said, though I was still confused.

"You don't need any assistance tossing my ass to the ground." I huffed and folded my arms across my chest.

He and Ryul laughed.

"We'll be gentle," Ryul said with a wink.

"Such gentlemen," I grumbled, stretching my arms and then my legs.

Venali smiled. "When you're ready, Your Majesty, attack me."

Alright. I could do this. I could fight them and not make a fool of myself. Right? Right. Maybe. Sure. Possibly.

Not a chance.

Raising my fists up to protect my face, I advanced, moving cautiously. I tried to keep them both in my sight, but Venali was making it impossible for me to see him and Ryul at the same time. He kept angling me in the opposite direction than I wanted to move.

Lunging forward, I tried to punch Venali, but he easily dodged and almost knocked my legs out from under me. I rolled away, coming up right next to Ryul, who had hopped down to join the fight.

Ryul tried to hit me, but I rolled away.

Now, I had a man on either side, both focused on me.

"How am I supposed to fight when you're on both sides?" I asked, keeping an eye on them.

"It depends on your opponents. I usually try to focus on one, attack him relentlessly and put him in his friends' line of sight."

"Easier said than done," I mumbled.

And, I doubted they would let that work for me here.

So, I decided to alter it a bit, and try to mix things up.

I ran at Ryul, kicking and hitting him as fast as I could. I felt Venali move closer, so I spun around, kicking at his stomach as hard as I could.

He caught my foot and jerked me forward.

I pushed off the ground, propelling myself up and onto him, wrapping my arms around his shoulders.

I'd expected him to release my leg, but he tightened his grip, preventing me from spinning around him like I had planned.

"While I enjoy hugs, I don't think hugging our enemy will make them admit defeat," Venali said, a wide smile on his face.

I shrugged, slightly out of breath. "It could work. Have you ever tried it?"

"No..." His smile became wry and his magenta eyes sparkled.

"Then, you don't know," I said.

"Come on, you brat," Ryul growled. "You need to take this seriously."

"I was," I said and kissed Venali's cheek before hoping down from his waist. "I planned to spin around him and choke him, but he didn't let go of my leg."

Venali laughed. "I knew you were up to something, but I didn't realize it was that."

"Let's go again," I said with determination.

We reset and tried again. This time, I didn't end up hugging him, but I still lost. We practiced ten more times, and each time I lost. But I was learning what did and didn't work.

"Break," Venali said.

I looked up from where I gasped for air. "Good idea."

Ryul pulled me up to my feet, and wrapped an arm around my waist to keep me up. "You hurt anywhere?"

"Nope. Just sore and tired," I said, leaning into him as we walked.

"You were improving, though," Venali came up beside me.

"Not much," I grumbled.

"You're better than you were this morning. That's all that matters." Venali offered a huge grin when we got to the house.

I gave him a smile, and then made my way to the bathroom for a nice shower.

After my shower, I felt clean but still exhausted. I trudged to Venali's office, and started writing my letters with Ryul nearby, scrutinizing my work.

"Ryul," Venali called.

"I'll be right back. Keep practicing." Ryul kissed my cheek and left the office.

I obeyed despite really wanting to follow and eavesdrop.

What could they be talking about?

Ryul returned a few minutes later, pointed to one of my letters, and said, "Fix that one."

I grumbled beneath my breath, crossed it out, and wrote it again.

Ryul nodded, satisfied.

"What did Venali need you for?" I kept my eyes still on my paper.

"Nothing important," he said.

I looked at him out of the corner of my eye.

He was smirking.

"You're a pain."

"You hate being left in the dark," he said. "Which is sad, because I'm not telling you."

"Whatever," I said with a sigh and gave up. He wouldn't tell me, so there was no use in pestering him.

"That's it?" he asked.

I looked at him. "What?"

He scowled at me. "That's it?"

"What's it?"

"You're not going to pester me more?" he asked.

I shook my head and focused back on my writing. "Nope. You won't tell me, so there is no point in asking again and again. We'll both just get frustrated."

He leaned back in his chair, staring at me.

Finished with my writing, I stood and stretched. "Done. What's next?"

"Go see Venali," he said with a dismissive wave of his hand.

I shrugged, happy to stretch my legs and searched the house for Venali. He wasn't on the first floor, though.

"Venali?" I called as I climbed the stairs to the second floor. In all this time, I hadn't been in any of the warlords' upper floors. I had no idea what they had up here.

From the looks of it, it was a bunch of bedrooms. I climbed to the next floor but stopped to take in the sight before me. It was a huge dining room, large enough to seat fifty people at least.

Venali sat at the end of the table, looking at a piece of parchment.

"Hey," I called out, heading towards him.

He waved.

"What are you doing?" I asked as I came to stand beside him.

"Looking over last-minute decisions," he answered.

I peeked over his shoulder. "For what?"

He folded it up before I could read it. "Amrynn said you are proficient in dancing."

I nodded. "Yes."

"Do you remember proper dining etiquette?" he asked.

I nodded again.

"Prove it," he said with a smirk.

I looked at the empty table. "Now?"

He rolled his eyes. "Downstairs, silly."

"Why were you up here, anyway?" I asked, taking another look at the room. It was larger than I thought. In addition to the table, there was a dance floor, a drink station, and a spot for a band. There were silver curtains hanging along the walls that gave it an ethereal feeling.

"You've never seen this room in Kydrus's house, have you?" Venali asked.

I shook my head. "I've never been above the first floor of any of the Warlords' houses. Except yours, today."

"Why not?" he asked, walking beside me as I headed for the exit.

I shrugged. "No reason to, I guess. I didn't want to snoop around."

"We don't have anything to hide from you. You're welcome to explore our homes."

I looked at him. "Should you be talking for the others like that?"

He chuckled. "We discuss a lot of things. And, we have known each other for over a thousand years. I can say with the utmost certainty that they would agree with me."

"If you say so," I mumbled, not fully believing him. Not that I was going to start snooping around their houses now that he'd said that anyways.

We walked down to the first floor, and Ryul was nowhere to be seen.

I scowled. Where could he have gone?

"He's on his border run," Venali said.

"What?" I asked, looking up at him.

"Every night he goes and runs around the border. It's to ease his worry, and for a bit of exercise," he explained, pulled out a chair at the dining table, and smiled reassuringly.

I sat without a response. Did it bother Venali that Ryul didn't trust him to protect me?

The table was set like it would be during a royal banquet. I stared at the three forks and a scowl pulled my eyebrows together. I had hated etiquette lessons. My instructor had been a mean old woman who smacked my hand whenever I had reached for the wrong fork.

"Silverware offends you?" Venali asked.

I snarled. "My prior teacher offends me."

He sat, tucking his napkin in his lap, and poured us both a cup of water. "Understandable. I've heard that etiquette teachers were the most hated."

"I had bruises from her. I thought I was going to have a scar on this hand," I said, examining my right one to see if there were any.

He took the raised hand, kissed it, and said, "Your hands are perfect."

"Flatterer." I gave him a coy smile while my cheeks heated.

He smiled in response and then said, "I've asked a few people to help with tonight."

On cue, two men walked in with platters of food. They set them down and left the room.

I put my napkin in my lap, took a tiny sip of water from my glass, and then smiled at Venali. "What a lovely presentation! You must tell me your chef's name so I might use him for a banquet at the palace."

His smile dropped a moment, but he quickly recovered. "Well, you're talking to the chef right now."

My eyes widened as I pretended to be surprised. "Oh, how lovely. You are such a well-rounded man. How are you still single?

I know a few girls who are very lovely that I am more than happy to send your way."

His smile dropped again "Okay, stop that."

I let my smile fall. "What?"

"Stop with this act," he said, with a slight curling of his upper lip.

I frowned, unsure why he was upset. "I'm just getting into the part. This is what I was trained to do."

"No. You don't have to do that. Just, be yourself. I just want to make sure you know which silverware to use and the other etiquette. I don't like this fake woman you're projecting."

"You realize that I'm going to have to act this way when we have royal events, right?"

"Why?"

"Because that's what monarchs do. We have to be nice, smile, and swap pleasantries with everyone. We have to pretend that we aren't bored out of our minds during these ridiculously long balls, and that the food their chef made isn't subpar to our father's, despite the fact he's not supposed to cook at all. This is what a queen does."

"You don't have to. You can just be yourself. Just because that was what they taught you, doesn't mean you have to follow it. You're starting the monarchy over. Be yourself. Don't be fake. Be the real you."

"The real me? I don't even know who the real me is anymore! I don't want to be a monarch. I want to live a peaceful life, but you five refuse. You five want me to be queen and rule Minloa. Fine. I've been trained for this. I will be queen, and to do that, I have to be fake. I have to smile even when I'm sad. I have to smile even if I'm fighting with someone. If someone calls me a whore and I overhear it, but they didn't say it to me directly, I have to ignore it. I've watched my mother do just that. I've watched my mother smile the entire night at a party, walk to her room, and then collapse and cry herself to sleep, not even bothering to remove her dress."

His eyes widened slightly. "You're going to change a lot in Minloa. Change how the monarchs are seen. Show the realm that monarchs are Seelie just like the rest of us. That you cry, bleed, and have fears as well."

"We are a beacon of hope. We are supposed to show the realm that even in the darkest of times, there is something to smile about. If you can't handle that, maybe you shouldn't be a guard."

His eyes darkened, and I immediately regretted my words, but they were already out there.

I picked up one of the forks. "This is for cheese and appetizers." I set it down, grabbed the next one and said, "This is for salad." I set it down and grabbed the last fork. "This is for the main course."

Shoving my chair back from the table, I left him sitting there in stunned silence, went to my room and locked my door for the first time ever, and lay on the bed with a sigh.

Why was I so upset? Because he was right. I could change things, but that felt like slapping my mother in her beautiful face. Like saying everything she did and endured was because she was too weak and pathetic to try to change things. My mother had been a beacon of light for me and many others. I didn't want to desecrate her memory just to make one man happy.

Then again, it would make me happier, too.

Not being queen would make me even happier, though.

"Elara?" Venali called softly through the door.

I didn't respond.

What would I even say to him?

He tried the door, found it locked, and sighed.

"Locked herself in her room?" Ryul asked.

"Yeah," Venali said. "I upset her."

"How?"

"Come on, there's food wasting in the dining room. I'll tell you what happened while we eat," Venali said.

"Okay."

I waited at least half an hour before heading to Venali's room to talk to him, but he wasn't there. I climbed into his bed, curling up beneath his blanket and fell asleep.

Sometime later, Venali climbed in behind me, wrapping his strong arms around me, and spooning his large body around mine. "I'm sorry."

I turned and kissed him. "No, I'm sorry. You're right."

"No, you're right. You will have to do things that I may not agree with, but I will have to bite my tongue. I'm just your guard. You will be queen and I have to defer to you."

I shook my head. "No. Please, don't do that. I don't want you to just be my guard. I want you to be—"

"What?" he asked, stroking his fingertips along my face and through my hair.

"My equal," I whispered. I wrapped my arms around his back and squeezed. "I want you guys to be my equals. Not just my guards, but my friends and my warlords."

"I can do that," he whispered and kissed me. "For you, I will do anything."

"I'm sorry I snapped at you," I whispered and kissed him back.

"I'm sorry I snarled at you." He left a trail of kisses along my neck.

"Venali, I don't like fighting with you."

He lifted his head to look down at me. "I don't like fighting with you either."

"Are we good?"

He smiled and brushed his lips across mine. "We're great."

I snuggled into him and fell asleep wrapped in his arms.

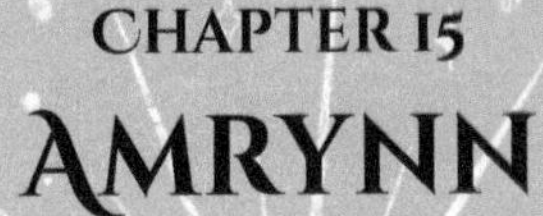

CHAPTER 15
AMRYNN

SHE WAS CHANGING ALREADY.

I was glad and yet I wasn't. The sweet, innocent young woman we had met was turning into a beautiful and strong woman.

I stood outside, looking up at the stars and planets that she could touch and manipulate at her will.

What must it be like to have that much power?

I was powerful, but her power was different, stranger. Seelie would bow to her as soon as she showed them that power. Some would fear her. Some would worship her. Some would want her.

A snarl lifted up my lip. I was already jealous at the thought of others touching her. Not my fellow warlords, though.

One of the stars moved. A shooting star?

No. It moved in multiple different ways. What was it?

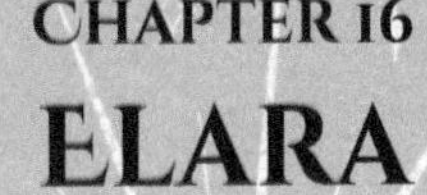

CHAPTER 16
ELARA

"Stop teasing me," I growled at Ryul.

He stood before me in just a towel, a smirk on his lips. "I'm not teasing you. I just got out of the shower."

"Put clothes on then." I squeezed my hands into fists, turning away from the drool-worthy sight that he was.

I heard the towel hit the floor and bit my lip to try to infuse my body with the willpower not to turn around and look. I'd come here to talk to him about my training and whether he thought it would be better for me to keep training with the warlords before I took power or if I was ready now. I hadn't expected to find him in just a towel, muscles and skin on display.

Warm hands slid along my bare arms. Ryul placed soft kisses along my neck, upper shoulders, and my jaw. "You need to relax, El."

I turned, keeping my eyes on his, and said, "I have a lot on my mind."

He smirked, and I watched as a droplet of water slid from his hairline, down the side of his face, and dripped from his chin to land on his chest.

I licked my lips, the desire to lick the droplet from his chest was so strong.

Ryul dropped to his knees, slid his fingers into the hem of my pants, and dragged them down slowly.

I gulped, watching as he undressed me.

He leaned forward, flicked his tongue out, and I gasped when it hit its mark.

"You need some distraction," he growled, stood, and crushed our mouths together.

I wrapped my arms around him, falling into the kiss.

He laid me down on the bed and slid inside me in the same movement.

I gasped into his mouth, arching against him.

He drew back and moaned. "I didn't realize you were so wet already. When was the last time you had sex?"

"I, uh, it's been awhile," I admitted.

He rocked back and slowly entered me again.

I may not have had sex in a long time, and hadn't had orgasms during sex then, but I had had orgasms from other things. But they were nothing like orgasms from sex.

I screamed into our kiss, which urged him to move faster.

I lost track of the number of orgasms I had before he withdrew, finishing on his towel on the floor.

Heat rose to my cheeks. I hadn't even thought about that. My hormones had overpowered my brain, which should have reminded me that pregnancy was not something we wanted right now.

He collapsed on the bed beside me, and I rolled over to lay my head on his chest.

He lazily stroked my arm.

"Is it always like that with you?" I asked.

He looked down at me and smirked. "No, it's usually better."

My eyes widened. "Better?"

He nodded. "Once you learn what really turns the other on, and what buttons to push, sex gets even better."

I didn't want to ask it. I shouldn't have asked it, but I did.

"How many women have you slept with?"

"Two," he admitted.

"That's it?" I asked, looking at him in disbelief.

He nodded. "I regretted both."

"Why?" I asked, petting his chest.

"Because they weren't you," he said. "It was during the time that I was mad at you."

"I don't care that you had sex with other women while I was gone. You had no idea what I was doing or where I was. Plus, we weren't a couple when you froze me."

"No, but I knew I would be your guard and future mate. I shouldn't have done it."

"Ryul, should I wait to become queen?"

He exhaled. "That's really up to you. I agree that you are learning really fast, and while there is still a lot for you to learn, I think you've learned enough to start as queen."

"I'm scared," I admitted.

He hugged me. "You've got the five of us. Everything will be fine."

I sat with Durlan and Ryul on the grass, telling them about the various planets and stars in our solar system. I'd made a full circle with the warlords and was back at Durlan's. I decided to give them all one more rotation, and then I'd take over as queen. All had agreed.

"That's a cold planet," I told them. "We wouldn't survive long there."

"The entire thing is cold?" Durlan asked.

I nodded. "Covered in ice."

"Could we go skiing there?" Ryul asked with a smirk.

Laughing, I shook my head. "We'd freeze to death."

Venali teleported in front of us, clutching his stomach, and coated in blood.

"Venali!" I yelped and rushed to him.

He dropped to a knee and lowered his head against my shoulder. "They've got Amrynn," he whispered.

"Who?" I asked.

Durlan placed his hands on Venali and began healing him.

"They came from the sky," he whispered.

"What?" Ryul asked, standing close by my side, his sword drawn.

"A huge machine came down from the sky. Beings came out, yelling in a language we didn't understand at first, but then they switched to our language. We tried to fight them, but their weapons are far more advanced. They took Amrynn and their leader said, 'Bring me the one who steals stars.'"

Me. They were after me.

"Take me to them," I said.

"No," Ryul and Venali said at the same time.

"We need to find out their intentions first," Durlan said. His brows were furrowed while he continued to heal Venali.

"They have Amrynn," I reminded him. "They could be torturing him right now! Take me to them."

"Not going to happen," Ryul growled.

I couldn't teleport, or I would have left on my own.

"Ryul, stay with Venali and Elara. If I don't come back, hide her," Durlan ordered him.

I grabbed his arm and stood as he did. "Don't go. Please."

Durlan bent and kissed my lips. "I'll return, my queen."

"Durlan," I yelled, but he disappeared.

"Let's get inside," Ryul said and helped Venali stand.

He seemed mostly healed, but he was still weak, judging by the way he leaned on Ryul.

I looked up at the night sky. If Durlan didn't return, I would just have to find a way to direct the intruders to me.

Ryul grabbed my wrist and dragged me into the house. "Get inside and behave, or I'll tie you up."

"You should tie her up as a precaution," Venali said.

"I find myself agreeing with you more and more," Ryul said to Venali. "It's disconcerting."

"Don't worry, I'm sure it won't happen very often," Venali offered with a weak smile.

"You need to shower," I told Venali.

"Will you be joining me?" he asked with a smirk.

Ryul growled.

My cheeks heated as I envisioned a wet and naked Venali.

Oh, I definitely wanted to see that, but...not tonight.

"Sit," Ryul ordered me as he walked Venali into the bathroom.

I sat on the floor of the hallway, my eyes glued to the front door as I waited for Durlan to return.

Ryul came out, alone, and shut the door behind him. "Let's go wait in the living room," he suggested.

"Will Venali be okay in there alone?" I asked as I stood.

"Interested in joining him?" Ryul asked, a small growl slipping out between words.

I looked up at him, my mouth agape. "No! I just don't want him to be hurt any more than he was."

Because of me.

"This isn't your fault," Ryul said, draped an arm around my shoulders, and he led me to the living room.

"How'd you know I was thinking that?" I whispered.

"Your expression, and the type of person you are." He squeezed me. "You have a good heart and will blame yourself for almost anything."

"Whatever," I mumbled since I didn't know what else to say. We sat on the couch, and Ryul kept his arm around me. Probably, because he was worried I would run off.

Venali came to the living room and sat beside me. His leg touched mine, and I tried really hard not to notice...and failed.

"Are you alright?" I asked as I turned to him.

He nodded, scowling at Ryul's hand between our shoulders.

My eyes started to droop.

No. I needed to stay awake.

"Did they have magic?" Ryul asked.

"No. Their weapons shot electrical charges and others shot fire, though."

Ryul pulled his arm from behind me and set his hand on mine. "You couldn't defeat them with your magic?"

My head fell forward, and I threw it back, opening my eyes wide. Why was I so tired?

Venali set a hand on my thigh, the heat from it was making me even sleepier.

"You're doing this," I slurred, realizing Venali was using magic on me. I looked into his eyes.

He smiled and rubbed his thumb over my leg. "Yes. I am."

"I don't want to sleep," I said, but my body fell to the side, leaning against Venali.

He tucked me under his arm and kissed the top of my head. "Good night, Elara."

"Jerk," I mumbled before his magic took hold and knocked me out.

I WOKE WITH A START, SHOOTING UP IN BED. SCANNING THE room to get my bearings, I realized two things. One, I was in my room in Durlan's house. Two, Ryul was asleep in a chair at the end of my bed.

Ryul's head was at an odd, extremely uncomfortable looking angle.

As quietly as possible, I slipped out of bed, only to get caught by my arm on something, and thump loudly to the floor with my arm still on the bed.

I glanced at my wrist to find a rope tied to it.

Ryul yawned and stretched. "I figured you would try to sneak out while I was sleeping."

"This is no way to treat your queen," I growled at him, and tried to untie my arm.

Ryul stood and untied it for me. "Protecting you is the most important thing. When we are back at the castle, and I know you're safe, I'll treat you like a queen."

"A queen is always in danger," I grumbled and rubbed at my now free wrist. "Did Durlan return?"

"I did," Durlan said from my doorway.

Before my brain registered my movements, I was throwing my arms around Durlan's neck and hugging him.

He squeezed me and chuckled. "I'll go on more missions if this is the type of welcome I'll receive upon my return."

"Did you get Amrynn?" I asked, stepping back from him. Strangely, I didn't feel embarrassed by the hug.

Durlan shook his head.

I marched to my dresser and took out a change of clothes.

"You're not handing yourself over to them," Ryul said.

"Yes, I am," I told him while changing. "I'm not leaving Amrynn in their hold."

"They will likely kill you," Durlan said.

I finished dressing and turned to face him. "I'm not abandoning him. I may have royal blood in my veins, but Amrynn is one of the warlords. He's done more for this realm than I have."

"He wouldn't want this," Durlan growled.

"I don't care. I'm doing this. You can't stop me."

"We stopped you last night," Venali said from behind Durlan.

"You'd rather keep me prisoner?" I asked.

All three males tensed.

I slipped on my shoes, and I wondered for a moment if it had been Ryul or Venali who had taken me to bed and removed my shoes.

I went to Durlan's office, grabbed the star from his desk, and turned to face Durlan. "Take me to them."

Durlan's brows were furrowed, but he held out his hand.

"No!" Ryul yelled and leapt towards us.

Durlan's hand closed around mine, and we teleported away before Ryul could touch us.

We teleported to an open field, where a monstrous silver thing sat. I had never seen anything like it. My mouth hung open as I stared. How could such a large thing even get off the ground?

"I'm against this," Durlan growled as we waited for some of the invaders to approach us.

Five guards, who appeared to be male, walked forward, holding strange devices.

"What do you want?" one of them asked Durlan.

"I've brought the one responsible for your missing star," Durlan explained.

"This way," the same guard ordered me.

I followed and wasn't surprised when they surrounded me.

"Elara!" Durlan yelled. "Let me go with her."

"Return to the others," I ordered him without looking back.

We approached the giant metal thing, and the ramp that led up into it.

"It won't eat me, will it?" I asked one of the guards softly.

They all chuckled.

"It is inanimate. It's just a bunch of metal," one said.

That helped me relax a bit.

Many more guards looked at me as I ascended the ramp. None said anything or did more than look, many of their eyes going to the star I carried in a jar.

Inside, the walls were white and seemed to be made from a different metal than the outside of the ship. They had lights illuminating the path, and I tried not to gawk at all the strange equipment.

We paused at a door, and one of the guards went inside.

I looked around and then bent closer to examine the suit of the guard beside me.

"You look like a kid in a candy store," he said with a laugh.

I bristled. "I may be younger than my companions, but I'm not a child."

"What are you? Twenty?" one of the guards on my left asked.

I nodded.

"That's basically a child to us, too," he said with another laugh.

"You age into the thousands, too?" I asked with wide eyes.

"Thousands? Did you say thousands?"

"Bring her in," the guard who had entered the room said, interrupting our discussion.

We filed into the room, which looked like a laboratory with really weird machines.

Amrynn sat in a cage, his face drawn and pale.

"Amrynn," I yelled and rushed to him. I slid on my knees next to his cage and reached through the bars to touch his face.

He opened his eyes and scowled. "Elara? What are you doing here?" The last words were said in a growl.

"Trying to save you," I whispered. "Are you injured? Did they torture you?"

"Most certainly not," a male voice said with undeniable indignity. "We aren't savages."

"Sedated me," Amrynn whispered.

That explained why he hadn't just teleported out of there.

I stood, blocking Amrynn from the newcomer's view. "What do you want?"

He was tall, somewhat muscular, but nothing like the warlords. His hair was dark brown, and his eyes were brown with caramel specks.

He held out his hand. "I'm Barry."

I stared at his hand a moment and then looked back up into his eyes. "I'm Elara."

His hand lowered to his side, but he didn't seem perturbed by my refusal to shake hands. "You're the one causing all this trouble?" he asked.

I held up the jar for him to see. "I didn't know my actions were causing trouble."

Amrynn discreetly placed his hand on the back of my leg. I fed him some of my power, so he could overcome their sedatives.

Barry leaned towards the jar. "Is that one of the stars?"

I nodded.

He tried to grab it, but I wrapped my arms around it. "Let him go, and I'll put your star back."

"You can't put it back from here. You'll misplace it." Barry frowned.

"What do you want me to do then?"

"Prepare for lift off," he yelled.

The other people on the ship began scrambling around.

"What are you doing?" I demanded.

Amrynn stood and tried to bend the metal of his cage apart.

"I'm going to take you to my universe, and you will put the star back in its proper place. Then, I'll return you to this planet."

"I can't just disappear! I have to tell the others," I yelled over the loud speakers shouting instructions. I didn't even know what they said, but it was loud and fast.

Barry scowled. "You're an important person?"

I nodded despite not feeling that way. "I'm royalty."

His eyes widened. "Well, how about if you write a note, and I'll send one of my people to deliver it?"

And tell him where the others were? Not a chance.

He noticed my scowl. "Or, we can leave your note below, so when they come searching for you here, they will find it."

I nodded. "Fine, but what about Amrynn?"

Barry frowned. "Who?"

I pointed behind me.

"I'm not leaving you alone on this ship," Amrynn growled. "I'm staying with you."

"He may stay. But, if he harms anyone, I'll cage him and sedate him. Understood?"

I nodded.

Barry handed me a strange parchment-like item and a writing utensil. I handed them to Amrynn.

"I'm not great at writing," I explained when Barry arched a brow.

Amrynn wrote a long letter, folded it up, and handed the writing items back. I transferred the items to Barry, who sent one of the guards away with it.

"How do we know you're—"

Barry interrupted me and pointed.

A screen appeared on the wall, and we could see the person securing the note on the ground before coming back in.

The ship shuddered and loud noises filled the air.

Amrynn gripped my arm through the cage, while I gripped the cage.

"Take off," Barry ordered them.

The ship moved, but despite not feeling it much, it still made me nauseous. My grip on Amrynn tightened.

"Elara?" Amrynn's brows were pinched with worry.

"Nauseous," I whispered back, turning away from him.

"That will pass in a moment," Barry said. "Once we are off planet."

Off planet. Something I had never in my life expected to hear. Being able to touch the stars and planets had made me long for the ability to travel through the solar system.

But not like this.

Not abandoning Ryul and the other three. They were going to be furious that I had left without them.

The ship slowed and the ride smoothed out.

I released my death grip and turned to Barry. "Let him out."

Barry tapped some keys on the front of the cage and Amrynn stepped out.

"Remember, no harming others," Barry said.

Amrynn stood between me and Barry. "I am here to protect Elara. Nothing else."

"If you'll follow me, I will take you to your rooms."

"We only need one," Amrynn said with a frown.

I looked up at him, trying to keep my mouth from gaping open.

Barry tilted his head to the side. "Oh? I didn't realize you two were—"

"We're not," I said a bit too quickly.

"Guards don't sleep in separate room when we're in hostile territories," Amrynn said.

Barry scowled. "Hostile? We aren't hostile."

"You were going to show us to our room?" I reminded Barry, not wanting them to fight.

Barry nodded and led the way.

Amrynn took my hand in his, threading our fingers together.

My hand looked so dainty in his.

"Are you alright?" Amrynn glanced down at me, but he was focused on our surroundings.

"Yes. No. I think so?"

He chuckled and squeezed my hand. "I feel the same."

I squeezed back. "I'm glad I have you here with me."

Barry stopped at a doorway. "This will be your room. You are free to explore the ship. We have surveillance that allows us to see everywhere, so please don't consider sabotaging the ship. I'll let you rest, but I would like to talk with you, Elara."

"What about?" Amrynn demanded.

"Your planet. Your abilities. I'm willing to trade information."

"I'll consider it," I said with a nod.

Amrynn entered the room and did a quick look. Then he tugged me in, and shut the door in Barry's face.

CHAPTER 17

ELARA

Amrynn immediately pulled me into a hug. "You stubborn, wonderful woman. Why did you come for me?"

I wrapped my arms around him, reveling in the fact that he was safe. "I couldn't let you get hurt because of my mistake. I thought they were torturing you."

"Careful, you might make me think you like me." He chuckled.

I looked up at him, scowling. After all this time I'd spent with him, how did he not know? "I do like you."

He smirked and traced my jaw with his fingertip. "I like you, too."

My stomach swirled in anticipation, but he just kept staring. I threw my arms around his neck, pulled him down, and kissed him.

Screw my boundaries. He had decided to stay with me while I traveled to a strange planet. He was handsome. And, he was my guard.

Without hesitation, he kissed me back, pushing me until my back hit the wall of the room, and then pressed himself into me.

I opened my mouth to him, letting him claim mine and then claiming his in return.

He drew back, stroked his fingertips down my cheek, and smiled. "That was an unexpected reaction."

"You should rest," I said and looked more closely at the room. There was a single bed, a door which I hoped led to the bathroom, a couch, and two chairs.

"We need to find food. We both lost some magic earlier."

He was right, but there didn't appear to be any food in the room.

"Stay here, and I'll go find us some food," Amrynn ordered me.

"No," I said immediately.

His brows pulled together.

"I don't want us separated. I don't trust those aliens. They could lock us apart in this huge ship and I don't know if I could find you." I shook my head and held his hand tighter.

He nodded and squeezed my hand. "Okay. Let's go together."

The hallway was relatively empty, save for a few guards, but they didn't stop us as we walked. This seemed to go on endlessly.

"Excuse me," I said to a passing human. "Where can we find food?"

"The replicator in your room makes food," she said.

"The what?" Amrynn asked.

She sighed. "There's a silver button on the wall next to your chairs. Push it. A table with a machine will slide out of the wall. You tell it what you want. It makes it."

"It makes anything?" I gaped at her. Where had they acquired these machines?

"Anything in our database that is edible," she nodded.

Amrynn took my hand and pulled me back to our room. I sat in one of the chairs and watched him use the machine.

First, he made rabbit stew, which I ate with relish. Then, he made sandwiches. An hour later, we were both full and satisfied.

"Sleep," I ordered him. "Venali knocked me out last night, so I'm well rested. You probably haven't slept since they captured you."

"Warlords are trained to function at full capacity with very little sleep. We could go—"

"Amrynn, go to sleep." I growled.

He sighed, but removed his boots, set his sword to lean against the wall beside the bed, and lay atop the sheets.

Within moments, he was snoring. He looked so peaceful when he slept. All of the warlords had such hectic lives. It was a wonder they ever got restful sleep.

What were the other three warlords doing now? Were they back to their normal courses of action? What about Ryul? Would he temporarily take Amrynn's place as warlord over Blustum?

Ryul was no doubt furious with me. Would he forgive me this time?

When I made it back, I would have to apologize profusely.

If we made it back.

If.

For all I knew, they would have me put the star back, and then keep me for experiments. Or execute me as an example to others.

No. Amrynn wouldn't let that happen.

But. They did overpower him before. It didn't seem too far-fetched that they could do it again.

I had to do everything within my power to keep Amrynn safe. This was all my fault anyway. I had to fix it.

A strange noise woke me. I opened my eyes, shocked that I had fallen asleep.

Amrynn still lay on the bed, his eyes closed.

Had I imagined it?

The noise came again.

Turning, I saw a red flashing light next to the door. There was a button near it, so I pushed it.

A screen turned on above the button, displaying the area outside our door.

Barry stood there, smiling. "Hello, Elara. I was hoping to speak to you."

"Let him in," Amrynn grumbled behind me.

I yelped, not having heard him get out of bed or put his shoes and weapon back on.

He smirked but made no apology.

"Okay," I told Barry and walked to sit in one of the chairs.

Amrynn opened the door and stepped back so Barry could enter.

Barry smiled at Amrynn as he passed and sat on the chair facing me. "Where do your powers come from?"

"We are all born with them," Amrynn answered from where he stood behind me.

"Most of your questions are better answered by Amrynn," I said. "He is much older than me."

Barry frowned. "He doesn't look much older? What? Ten or fifteen years at most."

"Try a thousand," I snickered.

Barry's eyes widened. "Thousand? You are over a thousand years old?"

Amrynn sat on the arm of my chair. "Technically Elara is, too, but she was frozen for about one thousand years."

"I'm not claiming those years," I grumbled. "I was a child when I came out of the crystal."

"You're technically still a child," Amrynn teased.

I flinched. Yes, I did know.

"What do you call yourselves?" Barry asked.

"We're fae. Specifically, Seelie," Amrynn answered.

"See...lee?"

"There are Seelie and Unseelie. The Unseelie are barbarians who use dark magic and revel in killing."

"They are your enemies?" Barry asked.

Amrynn nodded.

"Can Seelie become Unseelie?"

I perked up, curious of this answer as well. My parents had never explained the Unseelie to me. Just that they were evil, and I should run if one ever attacked. I had heard stories over the years, but no true explanation.

"There are some who are born Unseelie. There are some who are twisted and turn Unseelie. Turning is very rare. It has happened less than a dozen times."

"Can they become Seelie?" Barry asked.

"No," Amrynn said. "Once you touch black magic, there is no going back."

"What are your normal lifespans?"

"Four of five thousand years."

"Am I correct in assuming there are male and female?"

Amrynn nodded.

"Do you give live births?"

"Yes."

"What type of powers can Seelie possess?"

While Amrynn and Barry went back and forth, I sat there feeling uneasy. The Unseelie hadn't been seen in a long time. Why not? What were they doing?

"Elara!" Amrynn shouted.

I jerked away from him but had nowhere to go because I was in the chair still. "What?"

Barry frowned at me, and Amrynn looked concerned.

"Would you like our medical team to evaluate her?" Barry asked Amrynn, while staring at me.

Amrynn shook his head. "We don't get sick. She's just tired."

Had I done something? I had just been sitting there, hadn't I?

Amrynn scowled. "I'll be alright while you sleep. The nap I took helped."

I wasn't worried about that, but I stood and went to the bed. I cast a glance back at Amrynn, but he was deep in conversation with Barry again.

I tried to sleep. And the bed was incredibly comfortable, but my mind wouldn't shut off.

They wanted me to be queen, but did Minloa need a monarch? If they didn't want to be warlords anymore, I was certain we could think of something else. Why not find people that were respected and have the people of that sector vote?

Or, host a tournament and the top four victors would be the new warlords.

That idea had the most merit. Fae respected strength and power. A tournament provided entertainment and helped find the strongest among us.

Yes, once we got back, I would set into motion the tournament. After confirming with the warlords that they did want to give up their stations.

Once they were no longer warlords, I was no longer queen, they wouldn't need to guard me, so they could go find mates.

That thought hurt.

Thinking of them with other women really angered and upset me. I would have to get over it. I shouldn't keep the four of them...even if I wanted to, unless that was truly what they wanted. I didn't want them trying to stay with me out of obligation.

Barry left, and I rolled over to look at Amrynn.

"What's wrong?" he asked, coming to kneel beside the bed.

I sat up, crossed my legs, and looked at him. *Really* looked at him. His eyebrows were furrowed, eyes full of concern, his strong hands rested on the edge of the bed as he surveyed me.

"If you were free, what would you do?" I asked.

"Free?" He arched a brow. "I didn't realize I wasn't free."

"If you weren't a warlord. Or my guard," I added.

His eyes widened a second before returning to normal. "What?"

I sighed. "Come on, play along. If we were in Minloa, you weren't my guard or a warlord, what would you do?"

He looked at the wall behind me, silent, for several moments. I thought he wasn't going to respond at all.

"I suppose I would travel a bit, look for a mate, buy some land," he finally answered.

"I could make that happen for you," I whispered. "I could free you from all of this."

He stood and scowled down at me. "What are you talking about? What do you mean? You're going to fire me from being a warlord? You don't want me as a guard?"

The corner of his eyes were pinched.

Crap. I had hurt his feelings.

I stood and placed my hands on his chest. "Easy. I didn't say any of that."

He placed his hands over mine as he stared into my eyes. "I'm not leaving you. I will remain by your side until I die, or you force me away." He smirked. "I'll probably still stay close to you, even if you don't want me as a guard."

"I didn't say I don't want you as a guard."

"What did you say then?"

"That you have choices."

"Choices?" His left eyebrow rose.

I nodded.

"What if I don't like those choices?"

"What choices do you want?"

He raised a hand and rested it on my cheek. "The choice to touch you like this."

He kissed my lips. "The choice to kiss you."

He leaned forward again and nipped my nose. "The choice to tell you when you're being *ridiculous*."

I rubbed my nose with a scowl. "I just want you to be happy."

"I'd be a lot happier if we were on Minloa right now," he grumbled.

I leaned into him, and he wrapped his arms around me. "Me, too."

We stood like that for a while, and then I stepped back and went to the replicator to make more food.

"Did you find out anything from Barry?" I asked as I ordered food for us both.

"They are called humans. They live on a planet called Earth. Their average life span is eighty-five years. They tend to have a single mate, who they stay with for life. They do not have the same issues we do with male to female ratios. They use science to create their machines. They have weapons that shoot pieces of metal thousands of feet in a second."

My mouth dropped open. He had found out a lot. And, some of it was terrifying information.

"They're actually a very weak being. The only way they've survived so long is because of their weapons and science."

"Their weapons sound insane," I whispered.

His arms wrapped around me from behind. "We'll get through this."

I hoped so.

We ate in silence, both of our minds focused on other things.

Once he finished, Amrynn stood and said, "I'm going to continue training you while we are here."

"What type of training?" I asked as I stood as well.

"Everything I can possibly think of. We don't know how long we will be here. So, I want to give you a crash course on everything you didn't learn while on Minloa. If we have more time, I'll expand on certain areas."

I nodded. "Okay."

He frowned as he examined our room. "We need a different space. Come, we will go explore and find a place to train."

We walked for what felt like an hour and came to an intersection. There were signs, but I couldn't read them.

Amrynn turned right and pushed open a door, waiting for me to follow. Hopefully, he would remember how to get back to our room like he did earlier.

Inside the doors was another hallway, but it was thankfully shorter than the previous one and led to a large flat area with blue colored floors.

Amrynn knelt and touched the floor. "Mats," he said. "Perfect."

About a dozen people were in the room. Some were sparring, but most were lounging about, talking with each other.

Amrynn walked to an open spot and turned to face me. "Ready?"

"For wh—"

He charged me and knocked me on my back.

"I wasn't ready," I growled at him.

"Your enemies won't wait for you to be ready," he said and stood.

I stood quickly, put my hands up, and faced him.

He scowled and charged again.

I sidestepped and punched his stomach.

He grabbed my arm, twisted it up behind my back, and snarled.

I snarled back and spun out of his hold, kicking his chin.

He leaned back, so my kick only clipped him.

"You're better than I thought you would be," he said as he released me.

"I've been in my fair share of fights in Linta. And, I did train with Venali. Plus, you're holding back."

He was holding back *a lot*.

"I'm trying to avoid hurting you," he said, brows furrowed.

"I won't learn if you don't—"

He cut me off. "You won't learn if you're just constantly on the ground."

"You seem pretty sure you're the best fighter," one of the human men said, standing in a group, watching.

Amrynn didn't even bother turning to face him. "In this place, I am."

"Prove it," the man said, approaching us.

"Don't kill him," I ordered Amrynn.

The human took off his shirt, and I was temporarily put in a stupor as I looked at his muscular body. He looked as muscular as Ryul.

Amrynn growled at me, and I quickly averted my gaze.

Whoops. He'd caught me gawking.

Amrynn turned. "My queen?"

"Queen?" the man asked.

"Sparring with bare hands. Submission. No killing," I said.

Amrynn bowed. "Yes, my queen."

The man stared at me.

"Well?" Amrynn asked him with arms folded over his chest.

The man pulled his eyes away from me and nodded to Amrynn. "Agreed."

Amrynn unbuckled his sword and gave it to me. I backed up to the wall and leaned my upper back against it.

Barry walked in and stood beside me. "What's going on?"

"He challenged Amrynn to spar," I said. "Don't worry. I told Amrynn not to kill him and I have his sword."

Not that he couldn't kill the humans without his sword. It just made lesser beings feel better when they saw fae without weapons.

Barry perked up. "Wonderful. I was hoping to get footage of him fighting."

"It won't be a long match," I mumbled and bit my lip to hide my smile.

Amrynn and the human faced each other. The room was silent as everyone waited.

"Elara?" Amrynn called without taking his eyes from the man.

"Oh, right. Sorry. Fighters, ready?"

"Ready," the both called.

"Fight!" I yelled.

Before I had even drawn my breath back in, the man was on the ground, unconscious.

"What happened?" Barry asked.

"He punched him on the jaw," I said, hiding my smirk.

Amrynn knelt, pressed two fingers to the man's neck, and smiled at me. "He's alive."

"Did you use magic?" Barry asked.

Amrynn shook his head and walked towards me.

"Fascinating," Barry whispered.

Two people dragged the unconscious man off the mat.

"Would you be willing to fight more people?" Barry asked.

"I don't want him hurt," I said before Amrynn could answer.

"I swear it will only be sparring," Barry replied.

"Perhaps more than one at a time would be better?" Amrynn suggested with a smile.

Oh, he was enjoying this. Showoff.

Barry tapped on a metal rectangle in his hand. "Agreed."

A dozen more people entered, all wearing guards' uniforms.

"I'd like you to spar with our guest," Barry informed them.

"Four at a time, first," Amrynn said. He turned to me. "Pay attention to what I do. You need to learn to fight multiple opponents at once."

I nodded and sat cross-legged with his sword resting on my lap.

The newcomers removed their jackets and rolled up their shirt sleeves.

Four stood in a circle around Amrynn.

Amrynn bowed to me.

"Ready? Fight!" Barry yelled.

Two men fell as Amrynn darted between them and hit the back of their necks. The other two gaped, and then lunged sideways away from him as he ran at them.

"No magic!" I ordered him as he headed towards one.

Amrynn's leg shot out, and the man fell once it connected with his cheek.

The last man faced Amrynn with his hands raised, no fear showing.

Amrynn tilted his head as he examined him, and then he swept the man's legs out from under him and wrapped his arms around his neck.

The man tapped Amrynn's arm, and Amrynn released him.

"You're holding back," I said, my eyes wide.

Amrynn scowled. "You said not to kill them. If I move at full speed, I'll break their bones and probably kill them."

I dipped my head. Fair enough. He was most likely right.

"What about you?" Barry asked as he turned to face me. "Are females of your species as strong?"

"Most, yes. But, not me," I admitted.

"Would you be willing to spar?" Barry asked.

"No," Amrynn growled and marched towards us.

"He is my guard," I told Barry. "The moment he sees me in danger, the logical side of his brain shuts off, and he will attack anyone he views as a threat, or who has hurt me."

Amrynn stopped, folded his arms over his chest, and glared. "I am not controlled by my instincts. I'm not a young boy."

I smirked. Hook. Line. Sinker.

"Then, let me spar."

His lips twitched in a snarl. "No weapons."

I held out his sword and then gave him mine.

Once on the mat, the first guy Amrynn had knocked out stepped forward. "I'll spar with her."

Barry's wide smile was telling.

"You rank high in your military?" I asked.

The man smiled. "Yes."

I nodded. "Very well. No weapons, and submission or knock out."

"Agreed," the man said.

After stretching, I took a fighter's stance and said, "Ready."

The man looked at Barry, who nodded.

He moved quickly, but not as fast as my males could. I spun around his punch, ducked his back hand, kicked his legs out from under him, and sat on his hips, holding his arms down.

"Submit?" I asked with a smile.

Beneath my hips, his cock jumped.

My eyes widened, and I leapt away, heat rising to my cheeks.

He attacked, using my distracted state to get my arm behind my back, then tripped me.

I stumbled, spun to face him, and broke his hold before punching him in the stomach.

His abdominal muscles absorbed the punch, and before I knew what happened, I was in a headlock and unable to breathe.

I flailed as I tried to break free, but his hold was strong. Passing out wasn't an option. Amrynn would overreact. So, I tapped his arm in submission.

As soon as he let me go, I ran from the room and headed for our quarters.

Amrynn called after me, but I ignored him.

Once inside the bedroom, I quickly went to the bathroom, and shut and locked the door to keep Amrynn out.

I'd felt men's erections before. Sometimes they couldn't control them. I knew this.

What I hadn't expected was the lust I felt towards the human man. Or, my embarrassment.

"Are you injured?" Amrynn asked through the door.

"No," I whispered and slid to sit, leaning my back and head against the door.

"What happened? He didn't say anything, and I didn't see him do anything that should have upset you so much to lose."

"Just drop it. Please?"

"What happened?" he asked again.

That man wouldn't tell him. And, I didn't want to either. So, I stayed silent.

Amrynn sighed softly and then walked away.

Why had I reacted to that human? Was I so starved for attention that I would stoop to sleeping with a lesser being?

"I'm sorry," the man I had fought said from the other side of the door.

"Amrynn!"

"I'm here," he said outside the door. "He asked to come apologize.

Wonderful.

"You're beautiful, and normally I am better at controlling myself. I apologize for upsetting you."

Dammit. I didn't want them to think I was a child. I didn't want to be viewed as delicate.

"You've no reason to apologize," I told him, trying to sound nonchalant. "But I appreciate your apology."

Quickly, I turned on the water for a shower. I didn't want to see if they took the hint. I stripped and showered.

Being clean relaxed me a bit, but my hormones wouldn't quiet. There was one thing to do, and I was glad I was in the shower to be able to do it.

I reached down and touched myself, closing my eyes and

picturing my guards. I recalled the kisses I had shared with them and how sexy they all looked shirtless.

What would it feel like to have them lay atop me? To have their hands on my naked body? To have their tongues—

"Elara, we should—" Amrynn began as he entered the room. His eyes lowered to where my hand was, and they widened.

I was so close, and if I stopped now, I would be in a horrible mood the rest of the day.

"Amrynn," I growled.

"I, uh—"

"Are you going to just watch?" I asked, then bit my lip. That had come out more as an invitation than a scolding.

He dropped to his knees before me, the water of the shower soaking him and his clothes instantly, seared my lips with his, and slid his hand down the front of my body, not pausing until he pushed two fingers inside of me.

I gasped into his mouth, moving my fingers faster over my already sensitive nub.

He nipped my lip, then my neck. "What do you want me to do?" he asked. "How do you want me?"

Oh, sweet nectar! How could I answer that?

I wanted him in every way.

"What do *you* want?" I asked him back.

"All of you," he whispered in my ear in a husky voice. "But today, I'll just pleasure you."

"Why?"

"When I claim your body, it will be because you want me. Because you can't go a minute more without letting me spill my seed inside you," he growled softly as he pumped his fingers in and out of me.

I arched into his hand, my breaths coming in pants.

"I want you," I whispered. "I want all of my guards. It should feel wrong, but it doesn't. I want you all so much."

"We want you, too," he rumbled. "For now, I'll settle for making you scream and come on my fingers."

His head dipped, and he drew my nipple into his mouth.

I moaned, arched again, and then screamed as the wave of my orgasm, both from my clit and his fingers, crashed over me at the same time.

His fingers continued to move after my own stopped, bringing me three more orgasms before I finally felt sated. I fell back against the side of the shower.

He withdrew his fingers and licked them clean one by one. His eyes closed on the last one, as if he were savoring it.

Amrynn was a god compared to the humans. An immortal who could kill before they blinked. He was loyal to me, and I wanted him. I wanted all of him.

"You taste even better than I imagined," he whispered as he opened his eyes and looked at me.

"Why do you warlords have to be so perfect?" I breathed, my heart still thundering in my chest.

He smirked. "We are far from perfect."

"Can you help me stand?" I requested.

He picked me up, turned off the shower, and carried me to the towel rack. "He really was sorry."

"Who?" I asked as I dried off, out of his arms.

"The human you sparred with."

I sighed and dropped my head. "Can we just pretend that didn't happen?"

"For males, it is an involuntary reaction. Especially when seeing a creature as beautiful as you."

Clearly, we were not dropping the subject.

"I know it was involuntary," I mumbled as I dried my hair.

"Then why were you upset?"

I dropped the towel and glared at him. "I am supposed to

control my urges. I'm a royal. We are supposed to compartmentalize everything."

"Sexual urges can't be compartmentalized. Yes, you can control how you react, but not how your body does."

"Can we please drop this topic now?" I begged. I didn't have a change of clothes, so I put the ones I had worn earlier back on.

Amrynn didn't respond.

I turned, and my heart leapt into my throat.

Amrynn lay on his back, eyes closed, on the ground.

I rushed to his side, pressed my fingers to his neck, and checked for a pulse. It was there, strong as it should be, and he was breathing.

"Amrynn?" I whispered, gently setting my hands on his chest.

I looked around, trying to find something that could have hurt him, but found nothing.

Did they have devices in the wall? Could they inject us with sedatives without us knowing? Without needles?

"Amrynn, please don't leave. I need you," I whispered.

I didn't know what to do. There were no injuries to heal. His magic appeared fine. It was as though he'd fallen asleep.

Leaving him on the cold bathroom floor was not my wish, but I didn't want to move him, just in case something was wrong.

Gently, I lowered myself onto my side, rested my head on his chest to more easily monitor his breathing and heartbeat, and pressed myself as close to him as I could. Hopefully, my body heat would keep him a little warm.

I could summon Barry, but I wasn't convinced this wasn't his doing.

To keep from freaking out, I sang one of my mother's lullabies. I forgot a few words, so I hummed those parts. She used to sing to me all the time. Personally, I thought she just enjoyed singing, and I had given her a convenient excuse.

"That's a beautiful lullaby," Amrynn whispered.

I jerked upright to look down at him. "Are you alright?"

He nodded and sat up. "I'm sorry if I worried you."

I threw my arms around his neck. "What happened?"

He hugged me to him, stood with me in his arms, and carried me to the bed. "The others used a spell to communicate with me. It knocks the receiver unconscious to put them in a dream state." He climbed in beside me and covered us with the blanket.

"What did they say?" I asked, not wanting to let go of him yet. I lay on his chest again, his heart beat as strong as before.

"There was a lot of yelling and cursing. They found my note. They suggested we try teleporting, but I told them you were adamant about returning the star first."

Their anger was expected.

"How mad are they?" I asked in a whisper.

"They're not mad at you," he whispered back. "They're concerned for your wellbeing."

"Ryul is probably the angriest," I commented.

"He is very distraught. He made some impressive threats to me, should I fail in protecting you."

"Anything else?"

"Nothing important," he said as he began rubbing my arm.

"I'll get you back home," I swore, lifting my head to meet his eyes.

He smirked. "I'm certain that is my line."

"Minloa needs you," I said. "I'll get you home so you can live out your dream."

And, I would do whatever I had to, to get Amrynn back to Minloa.

CHAPTER 18
DURLAN

SITTING in the grass in front of my house, I stared up at the stars. Elara had been taken, and it was my fault. I'd teleported her to them. I had handed over my queen to those...people.

Ryul had attacked me, and I hadn't even bothered to try to defend myself. I'd deserved the beating.

Looking at the symbols on my arm, I drew in a stuttering breath. If she died, I would die as well. If she died, the magic would destroy me. And I would deserve it.

Failure.

I had never failed at anything in my life. Yet, one of the biggest moments, one of the most monumental times for me to succeed, and I had failed.

Venali had pulled Ryul off, but that hadn't done anything to calm his fury.

He viewed me as responsible for our queen's disappearance. I agreed.

I needed her to come back.

Rubbing the middle of my chest where pain had started as soon as she'd left the planet, I wondered what would happen if she and I did die. Would Ryul take over as warlord? Amrynn was gone with her, too. So, they would need to find a replacement for him as well.

Making a list of possible replacements for me seemed best. That way, Venali would be prepared.

Kydrus hadn't spoken to us since she had left. The pain etched in his face and eyes haunted me. He didn't share his emotions well, or speak much, but I knew he loved her. I knew he had loved her for several years. The moron just hadn't wanted to overstep his boundaries and risk her thinking she had to submit since he was warlord.

Our connection to her was pulled taut, separated by who knew how much space. She hadn't mentioned the connections, but they were there. If she didn't agree to be our mate, the connection would still be there. It would hurt to lose her as a mate, but we would still stay by her side as a guard, no matter what.

The connections worried me. Only one woman before had had connections like this, and if things were as they seemed, our world was going to change more than I liked.

I would endure. I would do anything for her. Just one more day with her was all I wanted.

"Come home," I whispered, looking up at the stars and planets above. "Come home, Elara."

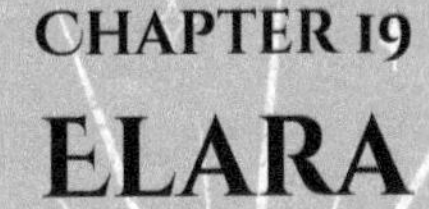

CHAPTER 19
ELARA

"You're not taking her blood." Amrynn snarled at Barry and the woman Barry had brought with him.

"It will only hurt for a moment, and it's not very painful," Barry pressed.

Amrynn stood between me and the humans, his sword drawn, and his teeth bared.

I'd caught a glimpse of his bared fangs when I had tried to step around him.

"What do you want it for?" I asked.

"To compare it to ours. See if there are differences in your DNA. Perhaps an extra or different chain that gives you your magic," Barry said as matter-of-fact but his wide eyes remained on Amrynn.

"No. You'll use her blood for experiments. You might try cloning her," Amrynn snapped.

"The last thing we need is two of me," I grumbled.

"We wouldn't clone her. We outlawed that practice decades ago."

Barry was trying to sound convincing, but even I could tell he was hiding something from us.

"No," I said. "Final answer."

Barry let out a long sigh. "If you reconsider, do let me know."

Amrynn didn't relax until they had left the room and walked several feet down the hallway.

"He's hiding something," I whispered.

Amrynn sheathed his sword and turned to face me. "Immortality."

"Huh?" I sat in one of the chairs and he sat across from me.

"They are a short-lived species. He wants to tamper with your blood to see if he can use it to lengthen their lifespans. If he succeeds, he will hold us prisoner, keeping us alive just to take our blood."

"You sound sure of this," I said with an arched eyebrow.

"It is what we might do, if we were in his place."

My mouth dropped open. "What?"

"It doesn't matter. He's not getting our blood."

His entire body was tense, coiled and ready to attack. I looked into his eyes and saw a predator. A gorgeous and frightening predator.

His gaze softened as he reached to take my hand. "What is it that has you flustered suddenly? You've gone a bit pale, but your eyes don't show fear." He rubbed the back of my hand with his thumb.

"You," I admitted.

His thumb still and eyes widened. "Me? I've scared you?"

I shook my head. "No. Well, yes, but no."

He scowled. "You're not making sense."

"You do scare me. You're a warlord, one of the most powerful fae in existence. Yet, I trust you not to hurt me." Had that made sense? Did I explain well enough, or just confuse him more?

His lips pulled up into a smile. "I'm glad I've earned your

trust. And, you don't need to be scared. Never. I will never hurt you."

Not my body at least. My heart...I had no idea what would happen to it.

Someone knocked on the door.

Amrynn sprung up, sword drawn.

I hadn't seen him draw it.

"What?" he demanded without opening the door.

"We have reached our solar system. Barry would like you to come to the captain's deck," an unfamiliar guard said.

After ensuring we had everything, we followed the guard.

Amrynn stayed close to my side, his sword still drawn. The hallways were filled with people, moving quickly.

The guard pressed a square thing he'd had hanging at his hip to a weird device. The device turned green, and two doors next to the device opened.

My mouth dropped open.

A dozen people examined machines with colored lights. Barry sat in a chair facing a huge glass window. Outside of the windows, I saw planets. I could feel the energy thrumming through me. I could destroy the planets with a gesture. The most immense power came from their sun.

"Ah, there you are. Come in," Barry beckoned.

I walked passed him, pressing my hands against the glass. "So much power," I whispered.

Amrynn set a hand on the base of my neck. "Don't give in to it. Yes, the power is there, but it is not for you to use."

"Can you return the star now?" Barry asked.

I could create a new star. I could multiply their planets. "I need to be outside," I whispered.

Amrynn knelt before me. "My queen, stay with me. Seal your aura."

"I don't know how," I said, my eyes fixed to the planets before me. Besides the power coming from the planets and sun, I felt another power deep within me. It was sealed and barely visible, but it was there. I had no idea how to coax it out, though.

"Can you get us to a planet where we can breathe?" Amrynn asked.

"Yes," Barry said and barked orders at the other humans.

"Do it, quickly," Amrynn said. He took one of my hands. "I can help, but it won't feel good."

"I don't want to," I whispered.

"You could burn yourself up if you use the power. You're untrained. It will overwhelm you."

"You don't know that for sure." I growled, showing him my fangs. I was queen. I ruled these stars. I could create and destroy.

Amrynn sighed. "I'm sorry."

My brows furrowed in a scowl. What was he apologizing for?

In a single movement, he pinned me to the floor, his teeth around my throat.

I gasped and went limp, almost dropping the jar with the star in it.

"What are you doing?" Barry demanded.

"S-sorry," I whispered. Tears sprang to my eyes and slid down my cheeks. The power was there but muted now. He had forced me to submit, and on instinct, I had reverted back to my slave self, sealing my power back inside.

He released my neck and picked me up, cradling me like a child with his hand wrapped around the back of my neck.

"Get us to a planet. This won't last long," Amrynn ordered them.

His touch was reassuring and not at the same time. I hadn't been forced to submit for over a decade. I had forgotten how much I hated it. I hated feeling weak and helpless.

"I'm sorry," he whispered. "I'm sorry, Elara."

"Put me down, please." I hardly recognized my own voice. It sounded so small and pathetic.

Reluctantly, he set me on my feet.

The guard I'd sparred with stood nearby, his hand on his weapon. Had he come to try to rescue me?

The chill I felt had nothing to do with the room. I wrapped my arms around myself and stared out the window, watching as we approached a planet with strange plants and animals. I carried the star in its jar and faced the guard. "Lead the way," I ordered him, barely keeping from adding a please to the end.

The effects would wear off soon, but for now I couldn't meet anyone's eyes.

Amrynn walked behind me, his presence reassuring and yet causing my shoulders to slump at the same time.

We boarded a strange ship and sat on seats with weird straps.

Amrynn reached a hand out towards me but lowered it when I flinched.

The smaller ship we were in flew out of the big one we'd taken to get here. we landed on the planet, and I tried to get the strap off, but couldn't figure it out.

I was about to use my sword, when the guard who always seemed to pop up, helped me.

The door opened, and I ran out. The dark night's sky greeted me.

"Do you know where it goes?" Barry asked.

I opened the jar, held the star in my fingers, and closed my eyes. Slowly, I turned, letting the star direct me.

There.

Raising my arm, I released the star.

"Brock?" Barry whispered.

"It's in the right place," an unfamiliar male voice said.

People cheered.

"Return us to our home," Amrynn ordered Barry.

"We have to refuel and restock first," Barry said, heading back towards the small ship.

"How long will that take?" Amrynn demanded.

"Are you alright?" the guard asked me.

I nodded. The magic beat through me, becoming stronger by the minute.

"You don't have to stay with him," the guard whispered.

I looked at him. "Who?"

"The male you came with. If he abuses you—"

"He doesn't."

"What he did on the deck—"

I stopped him. "He did it to save your home. There is a lot of power here. I could have destroyed this planet."

His frown was proof enough that he didn't believe me.

"He's saying it will take them a week to prepare for our return flight," Amrynn growled.

"A week? That's ridiculous," I shrieked. "I want to go home now."

"It takes time to refuel and restock. Plus, they will do a full inspection of the ship," the guard said.

My hair stood on end along my arms and the back of my neck tingled. Something wasn't right.

Barry beckoned us back to the small ship.

"Why are we getting back in that thing?" I asked, feet planted.

"To fly to our base. We landed far away, in case something went wrong when you tried to put the star back," he explained.

Amrynn and I reluctantly followed the guard and took our seats again.

The machine rose into the air with a roaring sound that made me grip the arms of my seat in fear.

Amrynn did the same.

They flew for quite a ways, and then landed at an area with

dozens of buildings, lots of strange machines, and too many humans to keep count.

We followed the group, and I didn't care how stupid I looked as I gawked at everything.

What did they do with all of these machines? Were they all weapons?

"We all need to go through decontamination," Barry said as he came to my side. "You step into a room and are sprayed with a powder that cleanses you."

"We will go in together," Amrynn said.

Barry shook his head. "You can't. you can go in rooms that are next to each other, though. They have clear glass, so you'll be able to see each other."

I didn't like this. Not one bit.

"Fine," I said, but glanced at Amrynn to let him know I was wary, too.

"It'll be fine," the guard said with a smile. "They blast some air and dust on you, and then you're done."

The powder wasn't what worried me.

"I can go first, if it will make you feel better?" he offered.

I nodded.

We headed into an enormous building and stood in line for the decontamination.

The effects of Amrynn's forced submission hadn't worn off yet. I could use some of my powers, but a very limited amount.

The guard went into a glass room, lifted his arms, and white powder sprayed him from every direction, coating him. The powder stopped and then air blew most of the powder off. He stepped out the other side, and smiled at me.

"I don't like this," Amrynn whispered to me.

I let my hand find his and squeezed. "Me neither, but we have no choice."

He snarled and went into the room on the left, while I stepped into the one on the right. The door shut and cut off all sound with it.

I turned and Amrynn's eyes met mine.

"Raise your arms," a voice instructed us.

I looked for the source but only saw the guard outside the door in front of me. He raised his arms in demonstration.

I obeyed, looking at Amrynn to find him doing the same.

"Close your eyes and mouth, and hold your breath," the unknown voice said.

I obeyed.

The powder sprayed, and it took all my willpower not to freak out. It coated my exposed skin and stuck to me.

The air blew a lot of it off. I wiped at my eyes and turned to find Amrynn lying on the ground in his room.

I hit the glass between us. "Amrynn!"

He didn't move.

I drew all of the power I could from their sun and released it as an explosion of fire. The glass walls and doors exploded. People yelled, and I took two steps towards Amrynn, but two unfamiliar guards held weird weapons to his head.

He still wasn't moving. I focused and heard his heart beating.

Relief surged through me.

"Release him or I will destroy your planet," I threatened.

"If you come with us quietly, we will keep him alive," Barry told me in a cold tone that was very unlike him. "If you fight, they'll blow a hole in his head. Which, I'm fairly certain your species can't survive."

That bastard. I would kill him. I would kill them all.

But...

I looked at Amrynn's limp body and growled. "If you hurt him, I will destroy everything in your solar system. Do you understand?"

"Perfectly," Barry said, and I could hear the smug satisfaction in his voice.

Two guards came for me, and one stabbed a needle into my arm.

The last thing I saw before I passed out was the guard shouting at Barry from the other room.

"You can't keep us here forever," I growled weakly at Barry.

My arms and legs were strapped down to a bed, a weird tube was inside my arm, pumping a clear liquid into my veins and another tube was inside my other arm, slowing draining my blood.

Amrynn lay in the room across from me, in the same predicament, but he was unconscious.

It had been a week since they'd captured us, and I didn't know how much more I could take.

They kept me heavily sedated, so I couldn't use my powers. Not that I would since they had weapons aimed at Amrynn constantly.

"Your DNA is amazing. It's similar to ours, but—"

I tuned him out. He liked to talk and wouldn't shut up for a long time, droning on about things I didn't understand.

He left a while later, carrying a bag of my blood with him, a gleeful smile on his face.

When we escaped, I would destroy this planet. I would crush them like the bugs they were, so they could never hurt us again.

Failure.

Pathetic.

Prisoner.

Slave.

I was all of those things.

Tears slipped down my cheeks, and I didn't bother to hold in my sobs.

I didn't want Amrynn to die because of me.

I didn't want to die.

Ryul, Venali, Kydrus, and Durlan would never know what happened to us. They would never get closure.

I would never see them again. They would keep me alive, to steal my blood, and I would never see my four guards.

These monsters could return to our world, capture the rest of my people, and strap them all to tables, stealing their blood, too. I had no idea if they would even stop at the adults. They might take the children, too. They could turn us into slaves.

I thought I had escaped being a slave.

Now, I had caused one of the warlords to become a helpless slave. A bag of blood.

"El...ar," Amrynn whispered.

"I'm sorry!" Tears dripped from my cheeks, to the bed, and then to the floor.

I couldn't be queen. I couldn't even protect one of my people.

Useless.

Powerless.

Pathetic.

If I could go back, take it all back, I would. I would have never touched the stars. I would have never met the warlords. I would have never gone to Linta. Ryul would have found out eventually that I was gone, and then he could have moved on.

I had caused nothing but pain and trouble for them.

If I made it out of here, I would do things differently. I would become queen, but rule differently than my father had. The warlords would be given a choice of leaving their stations or staying and becoming my mates.

I loved them. I loved each of them in their own way. I wanted to take them as mates, so that we could spend the rest of our lives together.

The lights went out, and then weird dim red lights came on, followed by loud sounds somewhere in the building.

The guard who'd sparred with me rushed in and began untying me and removing the tubes.

"What are you—"

"We don't have time. Just be quiet and I will help you escape," he snapped.

"They'll kill you. And, if I escape, I'll destroy your world."

He scoffed. "We deserve nothing less."

Finished unhooking all the things, he tossed me over his shoulder and moved to Amrynn.

"Why?" Amrynn asked softly.

"No one deserves to be treated this way. Especially not someone who returned our star," the guard said.

Free, Amrynn wavered on his feet, but stayed upright.

"Follow me," the guard ordered him.

Amrynn followed, his jaw set.

Was he really saving us or was this a ploy?

He pushed open a door and pointed, "Your swords."

Amrynn rushed forward, retrieving both of our swords.

We moved down a hallway but had to pause at an intersection when a group of guards rushed by. Luckily, they didn't spot us.

Once out of the building, he ran to the nearest machine, tossed me in the back, and ordered us to hide.

Amrynn covered me with a blanket and laid down next to me.

"Are you hurt?" he whispered.

"Sedated and drained of blood," I answered.

His lips pulled back in a snarl, but he didn't speak.

The machine made loud noises, and we headed away from the buildings.

Sometime later, he stopped the machine.

"All clear," he called out to us.

Amrynn tossed the blanket back and helped me out of the machine.

I looked around with a scowl. There was dirt and not much else. I could see the buildings where we'd been, but they were far away.

"I don't have a ship for you, or anyway for you to return," the guard said. "But I couldn't let them keep you like that any longer."

"They'll kill you if you return," I said.

He shrugged.

"Come with us," I said quickly.

Amrynn's head fell back and he looked up at the sky with a soft groan.

"I can't," the guard said with a sputter.

"I'm going to destroy this planet. If you don't come, you will die."

"I don't belong in your world." He frowned and shook his head.

"What's your name?" I asked.

"Jensen."

I hugged him and kissed his cheek. "Thank you, Jensen. I won't forget this or your sacrifice." I laced my fingers with Amrynn's, and said, "Last chance to come."

"What are you doing?" Amrynn muttered.

The guard stepped back. "I appreciate the offer, but I'll stay."

"Thank you," Amrynn said to him.

The guard smiled. "Take care of her."

I opened myself, drew in as much power as I could, and teleported Amrynn and I to the furthest planet in the system.

The planet was hot from being so close to their sun. I teleported us again as quickly as possible.

Amrynn groaned, curling around me.

"Hold on," I begged him. "Almost home."

My next jump took us to a freezing cold planet. I inhaled, and instantly regretted it. The longer we stood, the more frozen I became.

Crap. I needed to get us out of here before we froze to death.

My energy was already waning. I wasn't sure how many more jumps I could make.

Closing my eyes, gritting my teeth, and summoning more energy from their sun, I jumped out of their solar system and into our system, on the planet furthest from our sun.

We landed in a pile, Amrynn's body atop mine. He weighed so much more than I thought he would. Or, perhaps that was the gravity of this planet making him weigh more.

"Amrynn," I groaned, pushing at his shoulder. "You're squishing me."

He moaned but rolled off me. "Sorry," he exhaled.

I hopped us to another planet, closer to ours, but the use of so much magic was taking its toll on me and I was unsure where we were. Amrynn clung to my hand, but groaned.

I looked around. This planet looked familiar, felt familiar.

Oh, it was Pinolt! We were just three planets from home.

"I've got this." I gasped. Slowly, I wedged my shoulder and arm beneath Amrynn's, and jumped again, aiming for Sulma, the planet closest to ours.

We landed on a hill, sliding straight towards a bunch of jagged rocks.

I tried to teleport again, but my vision kept going dark.

"Elara," Amrynn groaned. "Elara, you can do it." He stabbed his sword into the ground, slowing our descent, and then finally stopping us when it hit a thick tree root.

I gasped in several breaths. "I'm sorry. I just need to make one more jump."

He looked down at me. "You've used too much energy. We should just rest here."

I looked down at the jagged rocks below us. "This is not an ideal resting place."

He chuckled. "Beggars can't be choosers."

I snorted and then laughed hysterically.

"Just rest for a couple minutes," he whispered, hugging me tight.

"You've been in and out of consciousness this entire trip. You could drop me," I whispered.

He growled. "I will not drop you."

"You could."

"I won't."

"But, you could."

"Elara!" he snapped, growling loudly. "I will *not* drop you."

I smiled, kissed him, and said, "If I don't survive, just know that I died happy."

"Wh—"

I jumped one last time, and the world darkened around me.

My eyelids fluttered open a moment later, and I stared at the ground rushing up towards us. We were falling from the sky towards Durlan's house.

I had teleported us to our planet, to Durlan's home, but in the sky above it.

"Whoops," I whispered. I looked over and groaned. Amrynn was unconscious. I didn't have the power to teleport us again. But I also didn't think I could teleport such a short distance. It felt like I could only travel across planets. "Amrynn! Save me!" I yelled.

Amrynn's eyes flew open, he took in our situation, gripped me tightly, and then teleported us safely down to Durlan's grass.

Safe. We were safe.

We collapsed on the grass, separating as we took in our safety.

My breath came in short and raspy gasps, and I felt the darkness encroaching again.

Amrynn sat upright, looking around a moment, and then he bellowed, "Durlan!"

Durlan, Ryul, Kydrus, and Venali burst from the house, and then froze when they saw us.

Ryul was the first to recover, running to me and setting his hands on my chest to check and heal me.

"You're alive," he whispered.

"Barely," I groaned, watching as several Ryul's shimmered around me. "There's three of you, no four. Four of you. I don't think I can handle four Ryuls."

"What happened?" Kydrus asked Amrynn.

"It's a long story. She needs rest and healing," Amrynn said and picked me up, ignoring Ryul's protest.

I closed my eyes, a smile on my lips. "I did it."

Amrynn brushed his lips across mine. "Yes, you did. You're truly amazing."

He lay me down on one of the couches, and Durlan took over healing me. Ryul stood behind the couch, looking down at me with a frown.

"How did you get back?" Durlan asked.

"Planet hopping," I whispered and then groaned. My entire body was sore, like after my training sessions with Venali. "It was hot then cold and then we got close and then we were falling." I giggled. "Falling."

"Stop talking," Amrynn growled at me. "Let me answer their questions."

I mocked him silently, mouthing back his words without saying them, a smile on my face while Durlan's body blocked me from Amrynn's sight.

Durlan smiled, while Kydrus scowled at me.

"How long were we gone?" Amrynn asked.

"A month," Ryul growled.

My mouth dropped open. "What? No, we were not."

"I was afraid time might move differently when we left our planet," Amrynn mumbled.

"A month? We were gone a month?" I asked, looking at Durlan and then at Ryul.

Ryul's jaw clenched.

Kydrus said, "Yes. You were gone thirty-two days to be exact."

I held up my hand, and Ryul grabbed it without hesitation, bending so he could place my palm against his cheek.

"I'm so sorry," I whispered, and then before I could stop them, tears streamed down my face, and my body shook with heavy sobs.

Durlan pulled me into a sitting position and wrapped his arms around me. Kydrus sat at my feet and rested his hand on my shin. Ryul placed several light kisses to the palm he held.

"I'm so sorry," I gasped between sobs. My brain was finally functioning correctly, which sucked since all of my emotions came with it.

Amrynn shoved his way in, grabbed my face between his hands, and stared into my eyes. "You have nothing to apologize for, Elara."

"You almost died...because of me," I sobbed, clutching his wrists. I sucked in a stuttering breath. "I couldn't protect you. I don't deserve you, any of you. I—"

"You did what you could," he whispered. "If it weren't for you, they would have killed me. Or, kept me as a blood donor on some distant planet. You rescued me."

"Jensen saved us," I reminded him.

"Because of you," he said and wiped the tears from beneath my eyes.

I shook my head but couldn't find the right words to say to him. There was something I could do, though.

"I need...stones," I gulped. I extricated myself from Amrynn's hold and wiped my face on my shirt. It took several breaths to calm myself fully.

"Stones? What kind of stones? For what?" Ryul asked.

"In my study," Durlan said. "I have lots in the third drawer from the left."

I hurried to his study and grabbed a handful of beautiful gemstones. "Perfect," I whispered.

"What are you doing?" Ryul asked.

I handed him four of the stones, keeping one in my hand. "Protecting our planet," I said, pushed open the door and strode out onto the grass.

Kydrus followed me out, right on my heels. "Elara, don't do anything that could hurt you. You need to rest. You need—"

"I need to protect Minloa," I snapped. "I won't let them come here. I won't let them take any of you and drain your blood. I won't let them use us as blood bags!"

Everyone except Amrynn halted, eyes widened at my proclamation.

I looked up at the sky, closed my eyes, raised my hand, and focused. Barry was far away, but I could still sense the sun and the planets. Since I had used power from them, I was even more connected than before. I grabbed the planet Barry inhabited in my hand, pulled it down, and shoved it into the gemstone. I opened my eyes and beamed at the glowing stone, with a single planet swirling within it.

"Holy shit," Kydrus gasped.

"She...a planet...what?" Ryul sputtered. "I've never heard of that before."

"Next," I ordered Ryul and set the current gemstone I held on the ground. He held out another gemstone, and I took it, then repeated the process until all of the planets were in gemstones. The last thing was their sun. I picked up the first gemstone, the one with Barry's planet in it, and pulled their sun into the gemstone. Now, I would use their sun and their planet as my power source. Like they had wanted to use my blood to fuel their research.

I turned and smiled at my guards. "Now, they'll never be able to harm us again."

The world tilted, and my eyes rolled up in the back of my head. I fell into a warm body, and fainted.

CHAPTER 20
ELARA

"You're mad at me," I whispered.

I had woken up a few minutes earlier, found Venali sitting in a chair in my room in Durlan's house, and stared at him silently. He hadn't said a word to me yesterday. He hadn't even touched me.

"I thought you were dead," he whispered.

I tossed the blankets back and walked to stand before him, surprised I was no longer sore. Durlan and Ryul must have both taken turns healing me.

I dropped to my knees and bowed my head. "I'm sorry, Venali. I made a huge mistake. It almost cost Amrynn his life. I'm so sorry. I understand if you don't want to be my guard. I'm willing to free you from that obligation. You can go do what you want. Start a new life. Get a mate. Do whatever you would do while not being a warlord or tied to me."

He slid to his knees before me, lifted my chin, and said, "You bow to no one, least of all me. I don't want to stop being warlord, and definitely don't want to stop being your guard. I was not mad at you for leaving. I was mad at myself for not being able to protect you. For failing to defeat our enemies. I thought you were dead. I thought I would never see you again. And, when I finally saw you, I was so overcome with emotions, that I couldn't let you see me in that state. We were certain you were dead. With no connection to you, and you gone for a month, we had no way of knowing what had happened. That was the worst part. Not knowing. Every night I looked at the stars, wishing for you to come back, wishing I could see you. Every day I ached for you to return."

His eyes gleamed with unshed tears.

"I don't deserve you," I whispered and rested my hand on his cheek, tears brimming in my own eyes.

"Please, don't leave us again. It was torture," he whispered and leaned into my hand.

I threw my arms around him and pressed my lips to his.

His arms wrapped around me, and he turned my frenzied kiss into a slow and deep one. One that left no doubt in my mind what his feelings were.

I pushed his chest, and he lay on his back on the floor, never separating our mouths. I lay atop him, reveling in his warmth a moment, the feel of his tongue sliding along mine, and then reality struck.

Kydrus knocked on the door. "Wake her up already. We need to meet," he said gruffly.

"Alright," Venali called back.

Kydrus's booted footsteps could be heard headed towards Durlan's study.

Venali stood, bringing me with him, and kissed me deeply. "I'm not quitting being warlord. I'm not quitting being your guard. I will stay by your side for as long as you will have me. And, hopefully, one day you might consider taking me as a mate. Okay?"

I nodded. I understood that was how he felt currently, but... "It's okay if you change your mind."

He sighed and rested his forehead against mine. "My beautiful queen, you constantly underestimate and undervalue yourself."

"I missed you," I admitted, and tears began leaking down my face. "I thought I was never going to see you again."

He hugged me tightly. "I missed you more than you will ever know."

"We should go to the others," I said and kissed him. I wanted to sit in his arms for eternity, but I wanted to see the others. I had something I needed to do.

He kissed the tears from my face, linked our fingers together, and led the way.

My four other guards instantly turned to watch me when I entered, their eyes glued to me like I might disappear again.

I sat on Amrynn's lap, kissed his cheek, and asked, "What are we meeting about?"

"How are you feeling today?" Durlan asked.

"I feel back to normal," I answered.

"You look upset," Ryul said, his brows furrowed.

Now was as good of a time as any.

I stood from Amrynn's lap, walked to stand beside the desk, and faced the five of them. "I'm going to take over being queen, but I'm going to do things a bit differently."

All of their eyes were wide, and mouths shut as they waited for me to tell them what the plan was.

"I will be queen, I will have warlords, but slightly different than before. My warlords will be my equals. I understand that you five may not want to be my warlords any longer, which is totally understandable. If you'd like to give up your station, there will be no punishment. I plan to hold a tournament for your replacements, to find the strongest in Minloa. However, if you stay with me, you will not only be my warlords and my friends, but, if you'll have me, my mates as well."

"You want the five of us as mates?" Kydrus asked.

I nodded. "If you don't want to be my mate, or can't handle sharing, I fully understand and there will be no hard feelings. I will take my place as queen in two months. I'd like to meet with you all individually to discuss your answers to my offer of being mates and your continued place as warlords. So, you can discuss amongst yourselves what order you come out, or just come when you want. I'll be outside waiting."

I left before they could say anything, shutting the office door behind me, then made my way outside and sat down. I had no idea what the five would decide. I assumed Ryul and Venali would stay with me, but I wasn't certain of Amrynn's response. Or Durlan's. He was so much more reserved than the others. Even more reserved than Kydrus, which was something I hadn't thought possible before.

I wanted them all. I wanted to keep all five of them, but I didn't hold hope for that outcome.

I had expected Ryul to be the first one out, but Kydrus was. He sat down in front of me and said, "I would like to accept your offer to be mates."

He was always so serious.

I smiled. "You're sure?"

He nodded.

"Thank you. I was actually concerned with what you would think and what your response would be," I admitted to him.

He leaned forward and kissed me. "I will follow you through time itself, Elara."

Kydrus teleported away, and Amrynn came out next. He knocked me to the ground and peppered my face with kisses. "You already know my answer."

"I do?"

He leaned back and arched an eyebrow. "You think after all of that, I wouldn't want to be your mate?"

"You suffered because I was too weak to protect you," I said with a frown.

He shook his head and said, "You teleported us across several planets just to get me home. I will follow you until the end of time."

I kissed him and whispered, "I love you."

He kissed my cheek and whispered in my ear, "I love you, too."

"Stop hogging her," Ryul grumbled. "You had her all to yourself for a month."

Amrynn smirked, kissed me again, and then walked by Ryul with a slap to his shoulder, not bothering to explain that, to us, it had only been a few weeks.

Ryul pulled me up and hugged me. "Do I even need to answer you?"

"Yes," I mumbled, but knew already that he wanted to be my mate. That we wanted to be mates.

"I want to be your mate. I want to be yours and I have no problem sharing you. Having a sliver of you is more than enough for me."

"Thank you."

Venali came next, kissed me deeply, and whispered, "yes."

I hugged him, resting my cheek on his chest. "Thank you."

"Durlan's last?" he asked.

I nodded.

"He's always the gentleman," Venali said and chuckled as he left.

I stayed standing, waiting for Durlan to come.

Several minutes passed, but he still didn't appear.

My heart fell. Of all of the men, I hadn't expected Durlan to turn me down. We weren't as intimate together, but I thought that was just how he was. Had I read him wrong?

I heard the door open and looked up.

"You look so distraught," Durlan said. "Did one of the others refuse you?"

"No," I answered.

He smiled. "You thought I was planning to refuse you?"

I shrugged.

He stopped before me, dropped to one knee and held my hand in his. "You, my queen, are too perfect for us to pass up. Refusing you would be like refusing a goddess."

I blushed. "Were you drinking before you came out here?"

Durlan tossed his head back and bellowed with laughter. "No, my queen. I'm sorry if I made you wait. I assumed the others would take longer. If you'll have me, I'll gladly accept being your mate."

To answer, I threw my arms around him and kissed him.

"Tomorrow we celebrate!" Venali shouted.

I turned in Durlan's arms, facing my other four mates, all smiling.

"Celebrate what?" I asked.

"Your birthday," Durlan said with a light laugh.

"You five are more than I could have ever wished for," I said. "I don't need anything else."

"Well, too bad, because we are still celebrating your birthday," Ryul said.

"What birthday is this? Twenty-nine or one thousand and twenty-nine?" I asked.

"One thousand and twenty-nine," Venali answered.

"You've been alive that long, just a bit frozen for most of it," Amrynn said and chuckled.

"Just a bit frozen," I said and rolled my eyes.

"At least you aren't sour like pickled cucumbers after being sealed up," Venali said.

Kydrus pulled me from Durlan and into his arms. "I'm just glad we were finally able to thaw that cold heart of yours."

I wrapped my arms around his neck and kissed his cheek. "Me, too."

"Can't we give her our group present now?" Venali asked.

"Her birthday has already passed," Durlan said. "I don't see why we couldn't. We can still celebrate her birthday tomorrow and give her our individual presents then."

"Now that she knows we have something," Ryul said with a smirk. "I think we should make her wait."

"That's just because you enjoy tormenting me," I grumbled and folded my arms across my chest.

"I vote yes," Amrynn said.

"Alright," Ryul said with a sigh. "I guess I'm outvoted."

"Close your eyes," Durlan ordered me.

I obeyed, but then started trying to open one just a bit.

"No peeking," Kydrus growled in my ear and then nipped it lightly.

I bit my lip to keep from making an embarrassing noise.

Four pairs of hands touched me, running along my arms, sides, back, and through my hair.

My mouth parted in a gasp.

A finger traced my lower lip, and I flicked my tongue out over it.

Five groans followed.

"You're all teasing me on purpose," I growled. "Because I can't open my eyes to see who is touching me where."

"Who said we're teasing," Durlan purred in my ear.

"Can I open my eyes yet?" I asked, my legs were started to quiver as my panties disintegrated in a pool of lust.

All hands were removed, leaving me feeling cold and vulnerable. I bit back a whimper.

"Open your eyes," Amrynn instructed.

I obeyed, then gasped.

Before me rested a silver crown, made to look like branches, and along the branches set jewels. They were the same jewels I had put Barry's planets in.

"You had this made for me?" I asked.

"Durlan made it," Kydrus said.

I turned to him. "You made this for me last night?"

He rubbed the back of his neck and smiled. "Yes. I thought the jewels deserved to be shown off by you. They are a symbol of your protection of our planet. And, I know you needed a crown."

"Can I put it on?" I asked. "Or do I have to wait until the ceremony?"

"Ceremony," Ryul said.

"You can try it on," Durlan said with a chuckle. "Stop trying to antagonize her."

Ryul smiled. "It's just so easy."

"Come on, you need a mirror," Venali said. He hooked an arm around my waist and guided me inside.

I leaned into him, inhaling his scent as we walked. The others followed close behind, and I resisted the urge to look back, to make sure they were still there.

"This isn't a dream, right?" I asked, swallowing a ball of emotion that swirled within me.

Venali tightened his hold on me. "You aren't dreaming, Elara."

Ryul pinched my arm, which made me laugh.

"Okay, I'm not dreaming."

Everyone crowded into my room, all five of my guys stood behind me. Durlan placed the crown on my head, and stepped back.

With the crown on, I looked regal, like a queen.

When I turned around, all five men were down on one knee, bowing.

"We offer our swords, our bodies, and our hearts to you, Elara," Durlan said.

"We will serve you for eternity," Ryul said.

"We will guide you and protect you," Kydrus said.

"We will be your friend and a shoulder to cry on," Amrynn said.

"And, we will destroy anyone who threatens you or your happiness," Venali said.

I believed them. I believed they would do all of those things and more.

"As heir to Minloa, I accept your oaths. Rise as my warlords, guards, and mates," I said.

Power thrummed in the room, and something sizzled on the back of my neck. My body shimmered a moment, my clothes morphing into a beautiful leather warrior outfit. Then, it disappeared.

I reached back, rubbing at the spot. There was no blood, but it was tender.

"What was that?" I asked, turning to face the guys.

All of them looked as shocked as I was.

"Was that..." Ryul started to ask, but trailed off.

Durlan examined Venali's neck, eyes wide. "I thought it was just a fable."

"What? What is it? What happened?" I asked, my voice near a shriek, but part of me felt it. Felt the power thrumming within me, the truth simmering in the back of my mind.

The guys exchanged glances, some type of silent communication happening.

"Hey!" I snapped. "Did you learn telepathy or something?"

"*You did, too,*" Ryul said, in my head.

I gasped. "Wha—"

"She's got her walls up really thick," Ryul told them, clutching at his head. "Getting that tiny message through to her was really painful."

"She may not know how to take them down, or how to create a wall that only we can go through," Amrynn whispered.

"Talk to me," I begged. "Tell me what's going on?"

"There's a story," Durlan began. "About the Goddess Amara and her Consorts."

Amara.

"I know that name," I whispered, pain tearing through my chest and head at the same time. I clutched at them, trying to quell the pain and pressure now present.

"You recognize the name, because it's your true name, isn't it?" Kydrus asked.

I swallowed, trying to remember. Hadn't I regained my memories? I remembered being raised by the king and queen. I remembered growing up with Ryul, and then being a slave. I had the scars as proof.

"I'm fae," I whispered. "I was raised here."

"Your body is, but your soul isn't," Kydrus said. "You've been reincarnated. You need to stop fighting it and let your soul fully merge with your current self."

I shook my head. "No. You're wrong. No."

I couldn't be a goddess. I couldn't be. Right? No. That was insane. This was insane. Had we been drugged? We were all hallucinating, right?

"This changes nothing," I whispered, trying not to panic. "We're moving forward as planned. Nothing has changed."

"Everything has changed," Venali whispered, eyes wide as saucers. "You're not only the queen, but also the goddess. Everyone is going to want to see her. Everyone is going to want to touch her. The Unseelie will want to kill her."

"We can't let anyone find out that she's Amara," Kydrus growled. "We can reveal her as queen, but not as the goddess. Not yet, anyway. We need her to fully accept herself first."

Each time they said that name, it changed part of me. I didn't like it. I didn't like it one bit! I wasn't her. I wasn't a celestial. I was just Elara, heir to the throne, orphan, former slave, mate of the Four Warlords of Minloa. That's who I was.

"Stop saying that name," I growled, but they didn't hear me, their focus on each other.

"If we announce her now, some will notice and could expose her. They could expose us. They will see her for who she really is. There are many with the power to see into one's soul. They'll see how old her soul is. They'll know she's Amara," Amrynn said.

"How is she hiding Amara within her? She is her, but we didn't see it until the bond formed. How is it possible that she is Amara?" Ryul asked.

"Amara didn't die in the tales. She just disappeared. She and her consorts all disappeared," Durlan said.

"If she is Amara, then we've got to help her unite herself," Venali whispered.

"Stop saying that name!" I screamed, throwing my arms to my side in frustration.

Power flared out around me in the form of a strong wind, knocking the guys onto their backs.

I gasped, my hands flew to my mouth, and I fell to my knees, reaching out towards them. "I'm sorry. I didn't mean to do that. Please, just...stop saying that name. It's not me. I'm not her. Please."

They sat up and then surrounded me with hugs and touches. None of them were hurt.

"Okay," Durlan said, his warm breath sliding along my neck as he spoke. "We won't say it anymore."

I took a shuddering breath. "I can't...it's too much. Too much."

"What is?" Ryul asked.

"The truth," I whispered as bits of information filtered in despite my best attempts to keep it all out. "It's too much. There's too much." I stood, extricating myself from the men. "There's so much to do. So much change. I need to find them. I must find them."

"What is she talking about?" Amrynn asked.

"Who?" Durlan asked.

"I think she's freaking out," Kydrus whispered. "We should knock her out and let her sleep this off."

"Why have they been hiding? What have they been up to? Will they even remember? Will he give me an audience? What if they attack my guards? I can't let them hurt my guards. But I can't go alone either. I can't let them get me. I can't let anyone keep me hostage again," I muttered as I headed to the living room, where I began pacing.

"Elara, what are you talking about?" Durlan asked.

"Everything is going to change. It's all changing. Changing. Changing. Just like before. It's all changing. My fault. It's all my fault." I cried and bit my lip to stop it's trembling.

Venali gripped my arms gently, staring down into my eyes. "Talk to us. Your mind is so jumbled, your aura is flashing all over the place. Tell us what you're talking about. Who are you going to see? Who might hurt us?"

I shouldn't tell them. They'd overreact. Ryul would want to hide me. Amrynn would want to run far away. He might even suggest the planet we'd teleported to before here, since he knew it could sustain us. Venali would want to slaughter them all before they even had the chance to hurt us. Kydrus. I didn't know what Kydrus would think.

"Open up to us, Elara. We are yours. You are ours. We are partners, remember? Partners talk to each other. Partners share everything with each other," Venali whispered, stroking my arms with his thumbs. "Tell us."

"Who are you wanting to go and find? Who do you need an audience before?" Ryul asked.

I looked at them and decided I had to tell them. They were tied to me now, bound to me in a way that no one else would understand. I wanted them to be my mates, but I hadn't wanted them to be stuck with me for eternity. A lifetime, yes, but not eternity.

"You're stuck with me for eternity now," I whispered. "You realize that?"

"We're fine with that," Venali assured me. "But we need to know what enemies are ahead of us. We need to know what threats we will be faced with."

"Who do you need to see?" Kydrus asked, a bit of growl and order in his tone. He towered over me, not to intimidate me, but in anticipation of protecting me.

I stepped back and turned so that I could see all of them at the same time. They were all anxious, their bodies tense with frustration and worry, perhaps even a bit of fear. I knew I was afraid.

I licked my lips nervously, and said, "I need to see the Unseelie monarch. I need an audience with the Unseelie Court."

CONTINUE ELARA'S STORY

Continue Elara's story with Book Two of Their Fae Goddess Series, EMPRESS OF THE GALAXY

ABOUT THE AUTHOR

Catherine Banks is a USA Today bestselling fantasy author who writes in several fantasy subgenres and has multiple pseudonyms. She began writing fiction at only four years old and finished her first full-length novel at the age of fifteen. She is married to her soulmate and best friend, Avery, who she has two amazing children with. After her full-time job, she reads books, plays video games, and watches anime shows and movies with her family to relax. Although she has lived in Northern California her entire life, she dreams of traveling around the world. Catherine is also C.E.O. of Turbo Kitten Industries™, a company with many hats including being a book publisher and Etsy store full of nerdy fun.

facebook.com/catherinebanksauthor

twitter.com/catherineebanks

amazon.com/author/catherinebanks

bookbub.com/authors/catherine-banks

MORE FROM CATHERINE BANKS

YOUNG ADULT PARANORMAL & FANTASY ROMANCE SERIES

Artemis Lupine Series

Song of the Moon
Kiss of a Star
Healed by the Fire
Battles of the Night
Artemis Lupine, The Complete Series

Little Death Bringer Duology

Mercenary
Protector
Little Death Bringer, The Official Coloring Book

Pirate Princess Series

Pirate Princess
Princess Triumvirate

ADULT PARANORMAL & FANTASY ROMANCE SERIES

Zodiac Shifters Paranormal Romance Series

Centaur's Prize
Tiger Tears
Lion About

Ciara Steele Novella Series

True Faces
Barbaric Tendencies

ADULT REVERSE HAREM PARANORMAL & FANTASY ROMANCE SERIES

Her Royal Harem Series

Royally Entangled
Royally Exposed
Royally Elected
Royally Enraged
Her Royal Harem, The Complete Series
The Demon's Fair
Her Royal Harem, The Coloring Book

Wings of Vengeance Series

Of Dragons and Cruelty
Of Minotaurs and Sacrifice
Wings of Vengeance, The Complete Series

Their Fae Goddess Trilogy

Queen of the Stars
Empress of the Galaxy
Goddess of the Universe
Their Fae Goddess, Complete Trilogy

Bonds of Madness Series

Sealing the Deal

Her Super Harem Series

Lucky Strike

VELLA ADULT PARANORMAL REVERSE HAREM ROMANCE

Shark (Season One)

The Golden Alicorns (Season One)

MORE FROM CATHERINE BANKS

STANDALONE YOUNG ADULT PARANORMAL & FANTASY ROMANCE BOOKS

Monster Academy
Daughter of Lions
Lady Serra and the Draconian
Of Sky and Sea
The Last Werewolf
Sybil Deceived
An Outcast Among Wolves

STANDALONE YOUNG ADULT PARANORMAL & FANTASY REVERSE HAREM ROMANCE BOOKS

Moon Academy
Claws & Wings

STANDALONE ADULT PARANORMAL & FANTASY ROMANCE BOOKS

Dragon's Blood

Last Ama Princess

Transforming Rose

Alys of Asgard

Phoenix Possessed

Stone Heart

STANDALONE URBAN FANTASY BOOKS

The Pawn

CHILDREN'S BOOKS

Calvin's Alien Adventure

MORE FROM DAISY EMORY

*Coming Soon

www.ingramcontent.com/pod-product-compliance
Lightning Source LLC
Chambersburg PA
CBHW030426310726
48979CB00009B/1635/J
9781946301659